Praise for *From a Low and Quiet Sea*

'An engrossing, unpredictable, beautifully crafted novel; Donal Ryan is giving us characters – their angles and their language – that we haven't seen in Irish literature before.'
RODDY DOYLE

'*From a Low and Quiet Sea* is brutal and beautiful. These carefully crafted portraits, deep and real, tied together, are fashioned by a true artist. I absolutely loved it.'
KIT DE WAAL

'*From a Low and Quiet Sea* is not only very cleverly constructed, but deeply moving too. I loved it.'
LOUIS DE BERNIÈRES

'This is a superb novel, from a writer building a body of work the equal of any today. His books are filled with love and righteous anger, most of which lurks darkly beneath the surface ready to explode.'
JOHN BOYNE

From a Low and Quiet Sea

Donal Ryan

Doubleday

LONDON · TORONTO · SYDNEY · AUCKLAND · JOHANNESBURG

TRANSWORLD PUBLISHERS
61–63 Uxbridge Road, London W5 5SA
www.penguin.co.uk

Transworld is part of the Penguin Random House group of companies
whose addresses can be found at global.penguinrandomhouse.com

Penguin
Random House
UK

First published in Great Britain in 2018 by Doubleday
an imprint of Transworld Publishers

A CIP catalogue record for this book
is available from the British Library.

ISBNs 9780857525345 (hb)
9781781620304 (tpb)

Typeset in 11½/15pt Electra by Falcon Oast Graphic Art Ltd.
Printed and bound by Clays Ltd, Elcograf S.p.A.

Penguin Random House is committed to a sustainable
future for our business, our readers and our planet. This book
is made from Forest Stewardship Council® certified paper.

To my dear sister Mary, my first friend, with love

Farouk

LET ME TELL you something about trees. They speak to each other. Just think what they must say. What could a tree have to say to a tree? Lots and lots. I bet they could talk for ever. Some of them live for centuries. The things they must see, that must happen around them, the things they must hear. They speak to each other through tunnels that extend from their roots, opened in the earth by fungus, sending their messages cell by cell, with a patience that could only be possessed by a living thing that cannot move. It would be like me telling you a story by saying one word each day. At breakfast I would say it, the word of the story, then I'd kiss you and I'd go to work and you'd go to school and all you'd have of the story is that single word each day and I would give no more until the next day, no matter how you begged. You'll have to have the patience of a tree, I'd say. Can you imagine how that would be? If a tree is starving, its neighbours will send it food. No one really knows how this can be, but it is. Nutrients will travel in the tunnel made of fungus from the roots of a healthy tree to its starving neighbour, even one of a different species. Trees live, like you and me, long lives, and they know things. They know the rule, the only one that's real and must be kept. What's the rule? You know. I've told you lots of times before. Be kind. Now sleep, my love, tomorrow will be long.

He stopped on the short landing and watched her through

the cracked door, shifting in her sheets to find the most comfortable way of lying. He could hear gunfire from the east, beyond the town, short of the front line, and he wondered if the shots were being fired in celebration, or in anger, or in tribute to some fallen warrior. He wondered if his daughter believed his lie – that the gunfire was the noise of a great machine that was being used to frighten birds away from crops. It was for the birds' own good, he'd told her: they'd gorge themselves till they were sick if they were let. He could hear her whispering to herself, or to her teddies and her dolls, ranged along the bed's edge, questioning: Could that be true, what Daddy said? That trees can talk to other trees? It must be true, or else he wouldn't have told me. I don't know if I'll tell my friends. Maybe I'll just keep it for me and all of you, and we can think about it just ourselves, and dream about it, maybe. Well, goodnight, babies. And she whispered each of their names in turn, and settled in the semi-dark, and there were only the sounds of the cicadas, and her breaths, and in the far distance another series of crackling bursts, like dry leaves underfoot fragmenting to dust. And the memory stung him again, so sharply this time that he almost sighed aloud, of how he'd hoped and prayed to God that she'd be born a boy. The moon was visible in the skylight above the landing and the stairs were drenched in its sickly light, and he felt a sudden hatred for it, the dead thing that circled one-faced and tide-locked above the earth, feeling nothing.

Martha was sitting at the dining table, her forearms extended along its heavy wooden top, her fingers stretched, a mug before her, her face tilted towards the steam that wisped from it, her eyes closed. He thought of how she'd sat in just that spot weeks before and spoken animatedly to a strange and dangerous man, how she'd smiled at him and laughed at things he said, a laugh calculated to please the man, to reassure him she was well disposed towards him, that she believed the things he said, the reasons he gave for doing what he did. Farouk had watched their interaction through the garden window as he'd smoked with the man's companion, a stick-thin youth of maybe twenty, with blemished skin beneath his patchy beard, the marks of pimples, of acne, the scars of the threshold of manhood. She'd wanted to speak to the man in charge, to get a sense of him, to see if he had solidness, a kind of ballast to his bearing. She was doing her best, he knew, to ease her terror, so she wouldn't opt to stay, to see if they could sit it out, this strange confluence of opposing certainties, this tiny Armageddon. The thin youth had sat in silence, looking now and then from the garden through the window towards his boss and the beautiful woman to whom he was speaking, and back to the woman's husband, and he'd grin, and raise his eyebrows, and exhale the smoke of his cigarette upwards in a thin stream, and nod, smiling, in approval, or reassurance, or just to be doing something, to mitigate the awkwardness somehow, the stilted silence that hung between them; it was impossible to say.

He had hated his wife in that moment, though he couldn't say for certain why. Because she was so able, maybe, to converse with a man so unknowable, a man whose word, he knew, could not be taken as truth. He felt humiliated, sitting outside his own house, on a stool beneath an olive tree, nodding back and forth with an idiot, inhaling foul tobacco simply because it had been offered to him and he'd been reluctant to appear cold or indifferent. He wasn't sure of himself: he wasn't able even to walk without considering his gait, the sureness of his step, whether his bearing seemed manly enough, whether his handshake was firm enough, without being so firm as to represent a challenge to the strangers, transmitted through their fingers and their palms. And he'd been careful to look away first once the greeting was done, and down at the ground between them, and this small act had caused a diminution in him, a terrible contraction.

He wanted her to stand in front of him and bow her head and lower her eyes and beg for his forgiveness, for closing out the deal he'd made, for taking the envelope of money from the shelf above the stove, for counting out the notes in little piles along the table, while he sat and smoked with a gurning boy, a sap-filled, leering youth. She'd gone too far: she'd only been meant to speak to him of her fears about the boat, to ask him of its type and provenance, and the size and experience of its crew. They'd agreed she would do this without him, so she'd be free to take liberties in her interrogation; if he was present he'd be obliged to rebuke her for speaking so volubly and insolently – they had no knowledge of the sensibilities of these people, of the way they might take things. And so he'd said to the one in charge, as they'd shaken hands in the doorway: My wife is afraid of the crossing, of the sea. She's never sailed before, but she has researched these matters. Perhaps you might allow her some technical details of the craft and of the course of our voyage, and of the skill of the crew, just to smooth the first part of our journey, to get us without drama to the port, you know how it is. And his mouth dried as he spoke the words, and the thick-limbed man laughed softly, and a light in his eyes danced, as he said, Of course, my friend, I know how it is.

His breath caught now as he thought of it on the moonlit

staircase as he descended, slowly, as quietly as he could, towards the soft billow of his wife's blouse where it moved in the delicately shifting air in and out from her skin, and a million prickles broke along his brow and down his neck and back and front, and down along his arms and legs to his feet and hands as his blood quickened and his heart beat in time with his clenching fists.

His wife stirred as he reached the lowest step, and she turned her head so her chin rested against her shoulder, and her face was tilted towards him but her eyes were fixed on some point far away, and he found himself checking her face and her eyes for evidence of tears, shed already or about to be shed, and he realized suddenly that he'd been hoping to see evidence of tears, of some kind of erosion of her alien strength, her seemingly unshakeable confidence in the rightness of their actions.

The war had come slowly, had accreted around them rather than exploded at their door. The police had turned to a militia. The town had filled with strangers armed with guns. A flogged woman was thrown one early evening from the back of a lorry onto the ground outside the hospital. She was bleeding heavily and her clothes were wadded and matted into the wounds on her back. There was a sign around her neck saying ADULTERESS. She was no more than twenty and one of the nurses seemed to know her, because she was crying as the semi-conscious woman was lifted into the hospital on a sheet, and she tried to straighten the arm that dangled at a strange angle from the makeshift gurney, broken perhaps in the fall from the high flatbed of the lorry, and the nurse was saying, O cousin, O cousin, what did you do? And one of the men who'd thrown the flogged woman from the lorry climbed down from the flatbed and walked towards the hospital entrance and addressed the people standing there. He spoke slowly and falteringly in Arabic, in a foreign accent, saying, This woman's life was spared because a fine was paid by her family. She is not to be touched by a man. If there is no woman doctor a nurse can be instructed through an open doorway from another room. From this day forward there will be two hospitals, one for men and one for women. The women's hospital will be set up in the school. Boys will be instructed elsewhere. Girls will stay at home. The man's face was red where it was not pasty white; his cheeks were puffed and his eyes were small and bulbous behind round spectacles; he wore a combat uniform and a rifle was slung on his shoulder and a long, curved knife like a scimitar was sheathed on his hip. He was German, Farouk guessed. He couldn't look away from him, this blotched, exotic specimen, this convert, filled to bursting with moral rectitude, with excitement at his new station, at the dream he was living. The fat German turned away and two of his comrades took an arm each and hoisted him back up on the lorry's bed and they were gone in a plume of dust.

She'd lost a third or so of the blood of her body and stock was running low. A senior doctor advised that the wounds be cleaned and sutured and salved with antibiotic cream and that she be hydrated and nourished and allowed to regenerate her own blood; she wasn't in dire need. The only female doctor in the hospital was nearly seventy and unused to dealing with wounds of this nature; this was a small and prosperous town, gout was a problem, and certain cancers were prevalent, and most people died of old age. We'll have to do as they say, she told Farouk that evening. We'll have to set up in the school-house, starting now. This patient can't be left here, and almost all the other female patients can be discharged or walked to the new building, and we'll pray to God to keep us from the centre of the storm. If we're faced with heavy casualties we have no hope. The flogged woman moaned softly and the nurse who was her relative put a wet towel to her forehead and then to her lips and she shushed her and said, Rest, cousin, and be quiet. Don't cause us any more trouble. Your wounds are already half healed.

And so the hospital divided its patients and its staff, and Farouk and the other doctors awaited the tide, and whenever he was able to he drove to the schoolhouse with whatever supplies could be spared. The women's hospital was bare, save for a row of low cots made from timber salvaged from the desks of the school. The female doctor and her two frightened, defiant nurses gave him a list of medicines and equipment they required each time he visited and all he could say was, I'll see. Maybe you could ask the Red Cross. But the fighting hadn't reached their town, only extended now and then in sorties from the south; it was a base from where the rebels launched attacks and regrouped afterwards, and the men's hospital had to treat the rebel casualties. And one of those evenings he had walked back to his car to find a strange, dark-eyed, heavyset man resting against it, who had said: I will get you and your wife and your daughter to Europe.

Here are the things that are known about you to the strangers in this town. Your wife does not cover herself. Her mother is a Christian from the north. Your father was some kind of apostate. You yourself are not observant and your home is unclean and your daughter is Westernized. He began to protest but the man dismissed this, saying, It's nothing to me, my friend. I don't believe in God. If He exists He has nothing to say to me nor I to Him. If ever I'm faced with Him I'll shrug my shoulders and say, I did what I did, you do what you must do. My business is transporting people from danger to safety. I believe in life, and I believe in making money, so that I may continue my work. I am an honest man. If you stay here your daughter will be taken as a bride for some so-called warrior and she will be raped. Your wife will be raped. You will be used until they have no more use for you and then you will be killed. Farouk knew that this man was in the business of fear, of extorting money from people and taking the guise of a saviour, but he well knew the truth that was buried in the man's exaggerations.

He felt foolish now as he remembered how he had searched the stranger's face and eyes as he had spoken, how he had tried to listen beyond what was spoken for the truth of him. How he had felt a childish pleasure when the trafficker had changed his tack from fear to flattery, asking him how it was to be a doctor, to be a man so educated and respected; how he had been touched when the trafficker had declared that if he ever had a son, and the boy grew up to be a man like him, a doctor with a beautiful wife, he would feel all his days had been worth living; he would die without regret. He remembered how he had revelled in the approbation of this thickset stranger, this dealer in flesh, how he'd been lulled and wooed by his softly wheedling voice, by the suggestion that the world somehow needed him more so than other men, that his wife and daughter had some claim above others on salvation.

His father had been devoted beyond reason to Mary, the mother of Christ. He paid tribute with the Christians at a church built in her name, on the side of a hill to the west of their town. He spoke of her in a soft voice, with reverence and a gentle, intractable love. She is all mothers, he would say, she is all women, all the best things of womanhood. There's no conflict here for us; she's sacred in our scripture, too. He thought sometimes his father had a kind of sickness when it came to the Virgin, that his devotion was a symptom of some profound malady, something that had worked insidiously into the core of him, and it was late in his father's life before he understood. The Virgin to him was the love of his mother, and the ghost of his wife, and the purest parts of his experience, and he communed with the memory of love in that tiny church, among his fervent Christian neighbours, and he wasn't alone in his strange devotion, in his curiously innocent idolatry. Many men and women of their faith attended Marian shrines, and saw no transgression in doing so, no affront or blasphemy. His father's many Christian friends and patients brought gifts of images of her, and the shelves of his study had been lined with them, and he'd given many hours to consideration of them, of their disparities and similarities, of the infinite shapes and hues of the Virgin, of her eyes especially, almost always raised, and her hands clasped always in prayer, her poor knees pierced by the stones that must have been there, at the foot of the Cross of her child.

You can't see inside another man's heart, his father told him once. They were sitting in a tiny stone church on a hillside above his grandmother's village, the first and only time Farouk had been inside a Christian church. A black-smocked priest led a circle of men and women at devotions, facing in turn each of the stations of the Cross, and he had raised a hand in welcome when they entered, and the low chant of the congregation and the cloying incense and the carved scenes of the Passion combined and formed themselves into a kind of waking dream, and the fear he'd felt that they were in some way causing offence to God by being there left him, and he rested in the wooden pew and listened to his father's whispered counsel. And his father said, But if you observe a man closely and properly you'll eventually come to know the shade of his soul. No soul is brilliant white, save for the souls of infants. But there are men alive who will do evil without pause, who are without mercy, and there are men alive who would rather die than harm another, and all of the rest of us fall somewhere in between. Be wary of prescription and proscription, of unyielding belief. All of it is dangerous; even something so lovely as this can turn to madness. And he talked on about the universe, and the oneness of all people and all things, how man was Nature's way of seeing itself, of feeling what it's like to be. And he said again to listen, to observe, to do your best to hear beyond the spoken, to see the quality of the light in another's eyes.

The crucified boy swung the argument. Farouk had been re-sisting until then, saying, Let's just see what the next month brings, whether this will pass. No one would dare touch us, and the fighting still is mostly far away; the front may even be retreating, not coming closer. Then the pooled blood in the crucified boy's bare feet, purplish and distended as though they might at any second burst like berries swollen on the vine, the plastic cable ties pulled to the last of their tolerance above his ankles; his curiously pale hands. Perhaps, he thought, the blood had drained from them, as they were raised above the line of his shoulders, and he'd been dead an hour or more when he'd come upon the scene. The dust of the market-place was settled that day, the crowd was thin and mostly still, people stepped softly where they stepped at all, and no man raised his voice or looked too long at the creature on the cross, the hooded boy who'd been a spy, it seemed, who'd spoken out of turn or sent a message from his phone or emailed someone, or transgressed in some way. He wasn't even sure it was a boy, just something in the way his knees were scabbed, and his shorts were belted low, spoke of childhood or the time just past it, when it's nearly impossible to keep the rules of men, to think of the world in terms of given things, to stop oneself laughing out of turn or acting on the impulses that flame and boil beneath the skin. A man stood at the cross's foot with a rifle cradled in his meaty arms, his feet planted in the dust, a black scarf tied around his lower face and one around his head, so all that was visible of his features were his eyes, and they were fathomless, and lightless, and dead.

Farouk, his wife said now. And then nothing. This was a thing she often did, as though to reinforce her own sense of his presence, of his realness to her. Always he used to say, Yes? Or, What is it? But he had learned with the years to stay silent when he sensed a certain mood of hers, a certain type of heavy quietness. Worry was passed now, discarded like a garment worn too long: they knew the ins and outs of the plan, of each stage of the journey, the rendezvous and routes and the vehicles that would be used. There was only a kind of cold tension left, a brittleness, as they each intently regarded the other, trying to hear the things unspoken. He'd left instructions in a letter for his closest friend, a doctor with no wife, whom he'd known since childhood, who'd shared a room with him at the university, who'd toasted him at his wedding, who'd smiled at his new-born daughter, his eyes filled with tears. His house could be used by the hospital, and anything in it, and his car, and he was sorry it had come to this. He'd measured the weights of his conflicting duties carefully, he told his friend in the letter, and he'd measured and measured again, and he'd mourned the time when such duties weren't in conflict one against the other but were all part of a good life and all given to the same end, but this now was how the world was, and he was left with no choice but to get his daughter and his wife to safety.

His wife's family had crowded into their house the previous evening, and her sisters, one a year older and one a year younger, had covered Martha's face with kisses as they clung to her, and they'd cried so loudly that he'd feared a passer-by would hear and think it suspicious that such sounds were coming from a house where no one had been lost, and deduce that they were leaving. Amira asked why her aunts were crying, and her grandmother said they were crying for joy, because they were so happy that their sister and their niece were going to have such an adventure. And she took Amira on her knee and said, When I see you again, my love, you might be a scientist, like your mother, or a doctor, like your father, or a baker, like your grandfather and me. Be happy, whatever you are, and remember how precious you are, and how much I love you. And Amira had smiled at her grandmother's words, and had lain in her lap awhile like a baby, and Martha's father had stood close beside Farouk, and they had watched the women's leave-taking in silence, until the old man whispered, Go with God, my son, and live long, and he had taken Farouk's hand in his, and the old man's hand was shaking hard.

Farouk, his wife said again, and he felt a sudden impulse rise within him to strike her hard across the face, and scream at her that this was all her doing, that he was sorry he'd ever told her about the trafficker and his invitations. He imagined himself standing over her, asking what the fuck she'd said to the man the evening she'd insisted on speaking to him alone, what promises she'd made him, what caused her to think it was all right to smile at him that way, to flirt with him, to giggle with her mouth covered like a coquettish adolescent, while he had sat outside looking in like a boy, like a penitent, on a stool in the garden, guarded by an acned fool. But it was quelled again as quickly, and he wondered at himself, at the things within him never felt till now. Perhaps, he thought, this is the way it is for everybody, at times of terrible pressure: maybe every possible version of a person can be glimpsed at once, maybe every man's true self is like a particle unobserved, assuming all possible shapes in any given moment, only fastening into one when it's called upon to be, to do. And he put his hand on her cheek, and was relieved when she took it in hers, and kissed it, and held it against her lips awhile, and told him over and over that she loved him, that she'd only ever loved him, of all the men who lived he was the only one who could ever make her happy. And he pitied every man who wasn't him.

He remembered London's low skies and humming streets, how the rain smelt in the mornings, sweetly earthy in the green areas and sharper, more metallic on the concrete and tarmac. He loved the sudden fogs, the way they'd roll in from the river and hang between the buildings, blunting the scape of the city, softening it, rendering it ghostly. He'd walk the mile or so from his digs to the university hospital and he'd smile at people he met on the path, and sometimes they'd smile back and bid him good morning. He walked with an umbrella because it seemed the thing to do, though he rarely opened it, and he went to pubs sometimes and watched series of small comedies played out between men and women who didn't know each other, and some of his fellow student doctors spent every spare moment in these mad pursuits, and he joined them sometimes but he never tried too hard. He wondered now how he'd feel when men like that were peacocking about his daughter, telling her tall tales, coaxing her, trying to impress her, to make her laugh, to wear her down so she'd agree to sleep with them. He was a man of the world, a progressive, almost a liberal. But still he heard a whisper inside himself, a soft voice, reasonable and measured, saying, Don't you envy those militants in a

The moon and the acacia tree and the jeep were aligned in the yard of his house, and there was a low vibration from the east and a sound of scuttling creatures from the scrub, and the man was standing at the driver's door and he was smiling, saying, I decided to drive you myself, brother. I feel a different kind of worry for you. I feel you have important things to do. Now, do you have the bribe money? Yes. Give it to me. There will be at least two patrols between here and the boat, and the moon is not our friend tonight: she's shining like a searchlight. You have been called to the home of your parents in the north because your father is dying. I am your cousin. Okay? Be sure your wife and your daughter are properly covered and that they have toileted, and tell them to be still if we are stopped, not to speak, to each other or to anybody else, unless they're spoken to first. Understand? And he said he understood, and his wife and daughter floated in their alien garb across the yard to the jeep, and the man hoisted their suit-cases, and his daughter asked again where they were going, why she had to wear this, and his wife said, Hush, my love, lie across my lap and go to sleep, it's still the dead of night.

He'd imagined that the journey would be quiet and tense, and that the night would be cloistering, oppressive, around them, but the earth was silver-lit and luminous, and the dust of the road was held down by the dew, and he'd forgotten how beautiful the land could be, when it swept and rolled and suddenly changed its texture and its shape, and he felt a longing for his childhood and his parents and the time when all his decisions were easy, or were made for him. The man drove mostly in silence but he spoke now and then in sudden bursts that startled Farouk as they began. He praised Farouk for his sense and said he hoped his colleagues and his neighbours would follow suit and leave. He half turned in his seat and smiled back and praised Martha for having a profession, a biologist, he said, slowing his voice to emphasize the word. The study of life. That is what I would have been myself, he said, had I had the brain! I only have wit enough for this, for driving cars and paying bribes and chartering sound vessels for the sea.

And one hour in, a truck appeared, stopped side-on in the horizon, and as they neared they saw that it was an armoured vehicle, marked with the crest of some foreign regime, and there were three soldiers strung across the tarmac of the road, two at either side crouched with their guns at their shoulders, aiming squarely at the windscreen of the jeep, and one in the middle, forward from them, his hand raised to halt them. Their driver rolled the jeep slowly to the checkpoint, lowering his window, smiling, and was told there was a toll now on this road, by order of the provisional government, and that the toll was calculated based on the number of passengers and the distance to their destination and the nature of their business, and the driver spoke in a low voice for a minute or so and he passed a sheaf of notes to the soldier, who nodded at Farouk and craned his neck to see the back seat and Farouk risked a glance over his shoulder and saw that his wife was still, her eyes were downcast, and his daughter was lying with her head on his wife's lap, and his wife had one gloved hand on her daughter's cheek and the other tucked demurely out of sight.

And at a wave from the leader of the soldiers the lorry was moved on a little so they could drive on with the white sun rising at their right, and at last they saw the glinting sea, and they stopped at a tiny slipway by a stunted quay and a gull bent itself to the breeze and screamed as Farouk and his wife and his daughter looked across a desert of water to the curve of the rim of the world. We wait, the driver said, and Farouk started to say something, then realized there was nothing to say, nothing to do but wait, and he was silent. A beach jagged away from the quay's left side towards a headland, and all along the beach were tiny knots of people, standing looking at the water and the path along it laid by the rising sun. Most of the groups were ringed by luggage, as though they'd arranged their possessions around them as protection, circles of totems strung along the sand containing souls, and all the things the souls could not leave behind in their old worlds. Some of them have been here days, the driver said, as though they were nothing to do with him, were the clients of less meticulous planners, less scrupulous fellows. He clicked his tongue and shook his head and checked his watch, and the solitary gull resumed its screaming as a tiny launch rounded the headland and its pilot wrestled it to its mooring at the quay and the knots of people loosened on the beach and hefted their luggage and made for it.

The boat was anchored out at sea, almost past the reach of a naked eye, and the launch was low in the water, but it was smooth and it didn't list or pitch, but rolled with the gentle swell, and his daughter's hand was resting on his arm, not squeezing it as it would if she were frightened. His wife gradually relaxed her grip on his forearm, and she turned her veiled face to the sun, and she hummed as they cut through the water and the sound of her matched the launch's diesel throb, and mitigated its ugliness, and he saw that their course dissected the sun's long reflection, and there was a sweetness that vied with the salt in the air, and the other people on board were silent but they seemed content, and men rested their feet on leather cases, and women smiled shyly at one another, and he felt a calmness he hadn't felt in weeks, or months, ever since the first days of the planning of their exodus. The pilot of the launch looked young, but he occupied his perch at the prow with authority; there was a practised assurance to his movements, a nonchalance to the way he scanned the horizon and adjusted his wheel to the roll of the swell so that they stayed as flat as they could, and it occurred to Farouk that all of the other passengers were well dressed enough and seemed respectable, and he decided that the trafficker hadn't lied outright when he said that this passage would be pleasant, that the ship they would sail on would be top-notch, that the crew would be experienced and professional, that his fellow passengers would be men like him, professional men, with good wives and well-behaved children, and there would be no riff-raff, and he felt a surge of pride that he was the kind of man who could arrange his family's escape, who had the wherewithal to get them to the West, and make for them there a life, new and better and absent of fear. He looked at the line of the profile of his wife's face, and he stirred a little so she'd look at him, and when she did he knew that he'd been right, that she saw him as a capable man, a strong husband and father, a saviour, and that she knew he'd allowed her to question the trafficker in the kitchen only to calm her own nervousness, that he'd humoured her. He breathed the crisp air deeply and he smiled.

This cannot be the vessel, he heard someone say, and there was movement from near the prow, and Farouk stood to look. The pilot was leaning down from his little bridge and he was answering the speaker in a fast voice, and the sun was flashing off the glass of his shades so Farouk could not make out his countenance, or tell if he was angry, but the man who had spoken was standing, and he was stabbing a finger towards the pilot's chest, and Farouk saw that he was holding in his right hand a small pair of field glasses through which he must have seen the anchored boat, and Farouk squinted against the sun and formed his hands into a shade on his brow and saw that the boat seemed small in the water, and single-masted, and to be made of wood, and was not at all as the man in charge had described, and he knew then why they had been taken from the shore on this launch: the traffickers could not allow the vessel to be inspected from dry land, when people still had the option of turning back, and setting out again along the road towards their homes. Farouk looked down at Martha and saw that she had removed her veil, and that she was smiling at him, and his daughter asked if they were nearly there, and said she felt sick in her belly, and asked if the big boat would be as bumpy as this one, and if she could talk to the girl over there, sitting with her mummy and her daddy and her brothers, and Farouk saw that the pilot now had a gun in his hand, a small rifle, and the strap of it was slung around his neck and the barrel of it was pointed down, and maybe it had been there all along but, for some reason, he hadn't noticed, and the complaining man was quiet now, and was taking his seat slowly, his eyes all the while on the gun's glinting barrel, and Farouk saw a jet-black seabird whirl and flap against the sun, and dive towards the water, and enter the waves with its wings sleeked back along its body, and he felt breathless suddenly, as though he'd just been running, and he sat and said, Of course, my little love, of course you may.

There was nothing then that could be done. He thought of all the things the man in charge had said, and all the questions he'd been a little too quick to answer, and the black cloth bag with drawstrings that he'd put the counted money in, and the tightness of his drawing of those strings, and the relief Farouk had felt when the bargain had been made, and the strange excitement that had fizzed inside him at the prospect of their adventure, and he felt a flushing burn inside his stomach at the memory of the vision he'd had of standing at the prow of a gleaming yacht, watching it plough the water cleanly, marvelling at its smoothness, at its litheness, with Martha standing beside him saying, Oh, how beautiful this is, how beautiful. And now they were here on this undulating sea, docking with a wooden tub, and the pilot of the launch was telling them to remove their life-jackets, they belonged to the launch, the ship's crew would give them more when they boarded, and he was holding the launch fast to the starboard side of the wooden boat by grasping a handle on its side, and he had lashed the launch loosely with an ancient-looking rope, and he was grasping a woman's arm as she stepped from the edge of the launch onto the bottom of a ladder that seemed to be fastened tight to the edge of the wooden boat's deck, and she was screaming to her husband that she was frightened, that it was too bumpy, that she wanted to go home, that this was no good, and her husband shoved her roughly from behind, and Farouk saw his field glasses, swinging from a strap around his neck.

He helped his wife and daughter up the ladder and onto the deck, and Martha stood with her hands on her daughter's shoulders and the girl stared in wonder at the mast that rose from the centre of the deck and the naked boom that jutted from it and she smiled at the little girl she had seen on the launch, who was half hidden now in her own mother's skirts, and she held her doll out from her so the little girl could see, and Farouk realized she wasn't afraid, that it would not occur to a child so loved and so protected to feel she was in danger, with her father and her mother so close by, that her trust in them was implicit and complete, that her love for them was perfect. He was grateful for his wife's strength, for her sub-version of her terror: she mortally feared the sea and had read of people fleeing in the past who had paid vast sums and been forced into dinghies, like sardines in a tin, and the dinghies had deflated and sunk with all souls, and she had accepted his decision that the people they were dealing with could be trusted to get them to safety, that they wouldn't dare lead people like them into danger, that this would be something more like a pleasure cruise, that the documentation they had been provided with, along with their own credentials, would mean a short stay on some small island before a transfer to mainland Europe, to some country that was short of doctors, and wasn't that every country in this day and age?

When at last the launch had been emptied of people and the small uncertain band of them stood on the wooden deck, the complaining man began an inspection of the craft. He walked aft and shook the rail and leaned over it so that Farouk thought he might fall in. His arse was large and so was his stomach and the rail was under pressure until he eased his weight back on his feet, and he removed his field glasses from around his neck and he replaced them, and he scanned the horizon with them, though for what purpose Farouk could not imagine, and then the man lowered himself to his knees as though in prayer but he put his ear to the boards of the deck, then rapped with his knuckles on the wood, and listened, as though for some reply, for some tone or timbre in the echo of his rapping that would reveal to him the seaworthiness or otherwise of the craft. Then he raised himself slowly and walked through his fellow passengers, who parted silently for him, and he made for the steps to the bridge, though they were cordoned with a chain, and as he raised a fat leg to breach the cordon the launch pilot shouted from his prow, Do not disturb the captain and the crew. They are sleeping. And he began to throw the luggage that was stacked at the centre of his small craft onto the deck of the wooden boat, and the complaining man leaned over the starboard side to remonstrate, but the pilot didn't answer him, or break from the rhythm he had established for leaning down and gripping a case or a bag and flinging it towards the passengers, and one bounced back from the top bar of the rail and splashed into the sea and sank quickly, and someone keened like a small child, and Farouk saw that it was a child, the girl his daughter had been smiling at, and her mother was weeping silently as she pulled her backwards from the rail saying, It's okay, it's okay, my darling, everything that's lost will be replaced.

When most of the luggage had been emptied onto the deck of the wooden boat, the pilot pointed to a hatch in the centre of the deck and commanded that they go below, and take a seat, and wait. And he raised his gun a little as he spoke, and his finger tapped the trigger guard in time with his words, as he said, Everyone go below, the crew will bring you water. It's dangerous to be seen on deck. And the belly of the boat was dark as pitch, and smelt of diesel and fish, and there were no seats, so the passengers lit the space with their iPhones and saw that there were people already there, sitting in silence, huddled, some with sleeping infants in their arms, some with young children who clung to their mothers, and Farouk could not discern their numbers, and the hatch closed above them, and there were voices, or a voice at least, raised, and a door opened and closed and opened again, and slammed hard shut, and there was shuffling and the motor of the launch revved high and throbbed away, and a long minute later the engine of their own vessel cranked, and he guessed the next series of mechanical expectorations to be the bilge pumps activating, and there was a door at the reach of his arm and he lit it with his iPhone's torch and he tried the wheeled handle of it but it was locked, or stuck tight, and he knew that it was the door to the engine room, and he breathed in and out slowly, and he searched for Martha's hand, and when at last he found it she said, softly, so that their daughter wouldn't hear, Farouk, my love, this is better than sitting and waiting for death.

The boat pitched and rolled and someone groaned sickly but mostly the hold was silent. And hours passed like this and Farouk thought of a story he'd read about Copernicus, the great observer, who pointed out the impossibility of taking a measurement of motion from below the deck of a ship, and how this observation on the measurement of relative motion was the same one Einstein made centuries later to explain the very fabric of space and time, and he wondered what kind of man he was to be sitting on the floor in the hold of a ship, like a prisoner, like a captured slave, having thoughts like these, useless thoughts, about things he only half understood, when he should be up on deck, questioning the captain and the crew, finding out why there was such a deficit between the trafficker's promises and the truth of this voyage, or at least securing fresh water for his daughter and his wife.

The sobbing noise was in his ears a while before he realized it was coming from his daughter. His wife had been speaking to her in a low voice, a story about a girl who'd been taken prisoner by a king who wanted to marry her, but he was old and very ugly and she would never love him, so he kept her locked away in a room in a tower filled with pretty things, all sorts of jewellery and clothes and musical instruments, and performers and clowns and storytellers were sent every day to amuse her but she spent her days sitting by a window feeding a tiny bird that landed on the sill, and whispering to the bird, and the king would visit in the evening but the girl would never speak to him, and he asked his best archer to kill the bird one day, and he watched from afar through a looking glass as a slender arrow pierced the bird's breast right there on the windowsill as the girl was whispering to it, and he watched as she sat there crying silently for hours, and her tears formed a pool around the bird's little body, and eventually the king regretted what he had done, and he tried to command all the birds of the sky to visit the girl, and to sit on her sill while she whispered to them, but the birds wouldn't listen, they wouldn't even stay still while he shouted at the sky and the trees, and the king's rage flooded through him and drove him insane and he asked all of his archers to kill every bird in the kingdom, and they obeyed him, because they were afraid of him, and the killing of the birds took years and years, and cost the king all his gold, and all his castles, because he had to recruit archers from all over the world to kill the birds, but eventually the skies of the kingdom were empty and bird-song was never heard again, and the king was a feeble old man living in a tiny shack in a silent forest, and the girl had long since escaped the tower and returned to her home and her family, and the king had long forgotten why he hated birds so much, why he had killed them all, why he had lost his very kingdom in the cause of their annihilation.

And Farouk wondered why Martha had chosen a story so sad, why she had made their daughter cry, and he realized that every other passenger had fallen silent and they were all looking now at his wife, and the only light there in the hold was from the slit along the jamb of the hatch above them and from the torches of phones, but he could see that some of the women and the girls had tears in their eyes, and some of the men had thoughtful expressions, and some looked angry, and the only sound was his daughter's low sobs as she clung fast to her mother, and the sound of his wife saying, Hush, love, it's not a true story, it's a fable, and its moral is how useless it is to blame others for things not being as we'd like them

Farouk enjoyed the telling of the story. Each time he told it something new occurred to him, some different meaning that could be ascribed to the girl and the tower and king and his war against the birds. Interviewers would invariably try to stop him at that part, tell him it wasn't relevant, that he didn't need to add this detail to his application, that there wasn't space for it, and he would pause, and he would regard them solemnly, and he would wait until they began to shift uncomfortably in their seats, or to exhort him to continue, and he would say, This is the most important part of my story, this *is* my story, and he'd laugh then, or sometimes cry, or sometimes both, a little, at the same time. Laughing and crying seemed equally ridiculous, equally useless. They seemed to be the same thing, ebb and flood of the same water, creeping inversions of each other, night, day, night, day, night. Sometimes he imagined the interviewer to be God, and the purpose of the interview to be to secure his passage to Heaven, to ascertain his eligibility for a place in the afterlife, to decide the quality of his treatment there. Sometimes he imagined the interviewer to be a child, and so he told his story from its beginning in the simplest of terms, in short sentences enunciated slowly, and sometimes he skipped straight to the story of the king and the girl and the birds, and the interviewers would shake their heads, and tell him that the session was terminated, that he shouldn't have made an application if he was unwilling to cooperate, to help himself, if he wasn't prepared to give a full and frank account of the reasons he was claiming asylum in their land.

He sometimes wondered if he lied. They supposed him to be lying, all of them. About being a doctor, about being smuggled in a fishing boat, about the reasons he had left his home, about his wife, about his daughter. Perhaps he had never had a daughter or a wife. They no longer seemed possible: the sea when he looked at it always seemed quiet; the storm that had thrown their boat from trough to crest to trough and splintered it to pieces didn't seem like a thing that could really have happened. The complaining man at the door to the bridge, shouting, Open up, open up in there, imploring Farouk to help him at the handle of the door, to help him break it down. The screaming wind, the screaming. The door giving way. Their bodies falling over each other into the emptiness of the bridge, the silent, soulless place. The flashing, bleeping box set by the wheel, locked to it. The auto-pilot and the satnav and the disgusted sea, lashing all its rage against the prow, and then against the stern, and then against the port side, and then against the starboard side, and then against the mast and boom and deck and hold and all the souls aboard the crewless craft, the small boat dumbly sailing to its doom.

His mind began to clear after a time, a time immeasurable, it seemed. He couldn't recall the date of their leaving, or the manner of it; he only knew, or judged from the softness of the air and the arc of the sun, that now it was early summer. There was short, prickly grass of a brownish green on the ground outside the tent. The beds in the tent were narrow and hard and arranged against its canvas sides in a rough square. Some of the other men lay on their backs and smoked all day, leaving only to queue for food and bottles of water in the morning and early afternoon and evening. For a week or so he was fully silent, watching from his bunk. Another man brought him food and water and addressed him as brother. There, brother, eat. There, brother, drink. And so he lay on his back on his narrow bunk in unfamiliar clothes: thick socks and heavy corduroy trousers and loose-fitting underwear and a white buttoned shirt over a white T-shirt and there was a neat pile of two sets of the exact same clothes beneath his bunk but there were no shoes. You have to keep an eye out when I am gone, brother, the man who brought him food and water told him. Your shoes have been stolen. Stay awake when I'm not here. These agencies are not well funded, and there are people here who should not be, and everything is pulled tight across a frame that grows each day, and everything is thinning and one day it will tear and disintegrate and we'll be left here to fight it out among ourselves, or this whole place will be levelled and we'll be bussed away to heaven knows where.

And Farouk spoke then, and the words seemed to press sharply against the sides of his throat, and to die in the air as they entered it. The man leaned closer and Farouk caught an odour of staleness and cigarette smoke and saw a raised rash on the man's neck extending down from his ear, and a white line of scar tissue cutting through his thin hair above the same ear, and the ear now was waiting for Farouk to attempt once again to speak, and the man's eyes were closed in patient anticipation, and Farouk sensed that this man had been alone a long time, was used to it, had been blown here by some careless wind, was dried to cracking and ready to crumble to dust. And Farouk said into the man's ear: I have to wait.

Well, brother, you can't stay here for ever. I am old, and I might die here. I don't mind dying here. I only pray it will happen in my sleep. We glimpse the next world in our dreams anyway; it would be no more than that, a dream from which I'd never wake. I feel a skipping and a murmuring in my chest some nights, a pausing and racing and pausing, and I feel sure my heart is coming to its useful end. I wouldn't have come here but I always dreaded being buried alive. It's my greatest fear. That's what drove me from my home. The thought of a great weight above me pressing down, of there being no room to move my arms or legs or to turn myself, of the total absence of light. My house was constructed from rammed earth and I stayed in it when everyone else was gone, my sons and their daughters to Europe and my wife to her grave, and every day the sound of the fighting came nearer and still I stayed until a line of Madayans passed my door on their way to the highway, some in cars and some on foot, drawing small wagons of children and belongings. Madaya has fallen, a man told me, and he described the bombardment, shells that fell and levelled whole streets, and people being buried in the ruins, people shouting from beneath the rubble. I set out walking then, and paid what I had to a man who gave me a seat on a dinghy, and the weather was clement and we washed up here.

And Farouk took the man's wrist in his hand and placed the ball of his thumb gently over the man's pulse and after a minute he said, You have an ectopic heartbeat. An extra spark. A tiny electrical signal is generated by your body that sparks the electrical function of your heart. You happen to have two sparks, and the extra one is intermittent and irregular and it kicks your heart out of step. It becomes noticeable when you are sedentary for long periods, as when you're lying down to sleep. It's nothing that can kill you. Potassium will regulate it, so eat bananas. Or perhaps you could be prescribed beta-blockers, but they can be severe and stymie cortisone production. My best advice to you, in order to keep your heartbeat settled, is to raise your pulse for a sustained period each day, by jogging or walking energetically, or swimming perhaps.

The old man laughed at this, a soft, almost noiseless laugh, a series of exhalations. Then he looked at Farouk, and his eyes were bright and there were wrinkles of mirth at the sides of them, and he said, You know, it's a funny thing. I knew you were a doctor from the moment they brought you here. Something in the way you carried yourself, in the way you greeted us when you arrived, or didn't greet us. Some feeling I had. I'm reading people's faces and their bearing a long time, though. It's never paid me yet, this skill I have. But so be it, some things just are. Why must you wait?

I have to wait here for my daughter and my wife. They're

with the other women and the children in some other part of the camp. That's how it's arranged here, isn't it? The children and women are separated from the men while suitable family accommodation is arranged, and then the processing of people's papers starts. I don't mind waiting here. I guess the other men are all here waiting too, while their wives and children set their places and prepare for the waiting-in. We have to be patient, all of us. There's no point in striking out against the tide. Martha has our papers and Amira is a clever girl and between them they'll arrange things and fetch me when it's time. I've never felt so tired in all my life. The journey, I suppose. I always worked long hours but never had to journey far before. Even when I flew to London and back again I slept both times. I was afraid of flying so took a sleeping pill each time. My father drove me to Damascus and collected me again. How easy it was then, to move about the world.

And he wondered why the old man stared at him with such a strange expression on his face. Why the old man's hand was resting on his shoulder now, and was squeezing his shoulder softly in a kind of gentle rhythm, why the old man was shaking his head slowly from side to side and saying, Sleep now, my friend, lie down and sleep. I'll stay here and watch over you and your spare clothes, and tomorrow I'll see about finding you some shoes. You need to sleep, brother. Farouk lay back on his bunk and the old man unrolled a coarse blanket from his own bunk, which was set at a right angle from the foot of Farouk's so that his pillow was almost at the edge of the doorway where the flap was bunched and secured with a short narrow chain and a hook, and Farouk thought how pleasant it would be later in the summer to leave the flaps tied back at night so the cool air would balm them and the soft sound of the sea would soothe them, and he hoped that he and Martha and Amira would have a tent together at the edge of the camp near the sea so that they would all three listen to the breaking waves and feel the gentle salty breeze in the evenings and watch the sun retreat below the line of the horizon and the galaxy begin to show itself, that splash of dirty milk across the sky.

And he wondered again and again as the days went on about the old man. His story of living alone in a house of rammed earth in a village near Madaya sounded like a lie, but Farouk didn't know why this should be so. It was a story like many others, but maybe that was why it had no ring of truth. What could the truth of him be? Farouk wondered why he was so interested in him. Why he toiled through the hours at a gathering of things: cushions and sheets and T-shirts and underwear. Why his accumulations waxed and waned – was he selling things? Was he a thief? The other men were not Arabs: they spoke a language he didn't recognize and the old man didn't speak to them at all, but still he moved easily around them and now and again presented them wordlessly with small gifts; without making eye contact he would hold up a garment or a blanket or a handful of cigarettes and one or other of the foreign men would accept the token with a nod or a trace of a smile. The old man seemed curiously politic, even in his silence, deferential to them almost, though without ever diminishing himself; in fact, he seemed straighter of back and to hold his chin higher when communicating in this curious way with the other men. There were five bunks in the tent. There were five men in the tent. Farouk breathed in and breathed out and ate the food he was given and drank the water he was given, and he visited the latrine beside their tent twice or three times each day, and he came to know that their tent was one of a great line of tents that stretched as far as he could see, punctuated regularly by prefabricated latrines and shower stands, and across the tops of the lines of tents, if he strained his eyes against the brightness of the sun, he could see the tops of grassy dunes and he could hear the breaking rolling waves and he supposed that the women and children were sequestered there, in a more pleasant area, where the sea view was more easily accessible and the children could play on the beach and climb among the rocks, and he felt happy that Martha and Amira were having this time together, this period of gradual adjustment, before they would regroup and continue their journey.

This mourning time must end, my brother, the old man said one day. And Farouk supposed the old man to have lost his mind. His arrhythmias perhaps had worsened and caused some coagulation and a blockage that may have led to haemorrhage – a minor stroke. This mourning time cannot go on for ever, the old man was saying now. This turning of your back on things. Farouk was lying on his side and the old man was sitting on the edge of Farouk's bunk and he was narrow, this man, twig-like: he had the bones of a bird and the drawn, leathery skin of something ancient, something long dead but cured, preserved. His stomach lurched suddenly, he felt bilious at the thought, and the weight of the old man's hand on his side through his blanket and his shirt seemed deathly, seemed infinite, seemed to be so heavy as to have stopped his lungs: he couldn't draw in air; he was drowning.

At last the man removed his hand and Farouk gasped and sat up in his bunk and the old man stood quickly and stumbled a little before righting himself. The three foreigners were standing at the far end of the tent and they were all looking intently across at Farouk and the old man and at something else, something that Farouk couldn't see. And the old man turned suddenly and inclined his head towards the three foreigners and he motioned sharply with his hand and they at once filed out of the tent, and Farouk saw as they left that they were barefoot except for the biggest of them: he wore leather sandals that were buckled at the sides, but loosely, and they made a sucking and a popping noise as he walked, as the soles of his feet pressed into the leather and compressed and released air with each step.

Again the old man said, This foolishness must end. And he was standing still and stooped, bent from the waist, and he had his left hand on his hip and his right arm was extended towards Farouk, and he seemed bigger now, somehow, to be looming, hulking, and Farouk imagined the old man's hand to be a hand that had held weapons, that had done terrible things; he imagined the hand itself to be a weapon, capable of tearing flesh and smashing bone. This turning away from things must end, brother. You have an obligation to live. You have an obligation to go on with your journey, to see the worth of the terrible price you've paid.

And Farouk could find no words for this old man, this poor creature who had lost his mind – had he been drinking saltwater? Had he succumbed to madness from the length of his wait, from the terrible monotony of his days in this open confinement, in this maddening rank of canvas tents? And the man was saying, It's not natural that you should mourn like this. There are many others hereabouts who've lost far more – a man a few tents down has lost two sons, two fine boys, one in the fighting and one on the crossing. Wives are easily found, especially by men like you, and daughters are easily made. And Farouk was on his feet and his hands were at the old man's throat and the three foreigners were back in the tent and they were dragging him away and holding his arms high behind him and the old man was backing away from him, pushing with his feet like an infant, and he had one of his clawed hands to his throat and his eyes were bulging from his face and his mouth was open and his features were contorted so that he looked crazed and demonic, and something crashed into the side of Farouk's head and the day fell suddenly to starless night.

He woke in a different place, a room with white walls, lit by a fluorescent tube. His head ached dully and his mouth was dry. Farouk realized there was a person present, a young woman who was sitting on a chair with her hands twined together in her lap, and her lap was level with his head, and she had an oversized sleeveless jacket on her small frame that was coloured a luminous orange, like a life-jacket, and she wore a light blue sweatshirt beneath that with writing on it but he couldn't make the letters out, and she had glasses on with thin frames and her eyes behind the glasses were blue and they were full of some unreadable thing, some kind of silent knowing, and she was smiling a little and her head was inclined towards him as though in expectation of something, some action or utterance from him, though he couldn't imagine exactly what.

He noticed standing by the door a bulky man, young, pale and blotched, in scrubs that seemed a size or two too small. He spoke in English to the sitting woman, but his accent was unfamiliar and his voice was too fast for Farouk to make out all of his words, and she nodded but she was silent still, and smiling still, just slightly, and the expression in her eyes was still of knowing, of holding something dread away in store, of fear of the dread thing, the terrible weight of it, the dead weight of it, and Farouk began to tell her she should leave, there was no need for her to extend herself like this, to stretch herself to breaking just for him; whatever it was she knew she needn't share, whatever news she felt she must break to him, about head trauma or contusions or possible concussions or delays or complications or refusals of consulates or countries or agents thereof to grant visas or mercies or passage or grace, or of lost identifications or lost purses or lost luggage, or bombed hospitals or dead colleagues or escalations of hostilities or conflagrations or annihilations or massacres or of the damage done to the cabin door when he and the complaining man had smashed it in just before they were knocked from their feet by the whirling storm, and again he heard the old man say: This mourning time must end.

And he was screaming now. For them both to go to Hell. To go and leave him to his narrow bunk and his wait, to his watching of the sun's widening arc and the sky's deepening redness as the summer stretched the days and shrank the nights, to his wait, for Martha and Amira to prepare their house, to arrange their beds and their table and chairs, because surely the accommodation given to families was more salubrious than this, surely there'd be tables for their meals and not their laps, and chairs to sit on instead of bunks, and a door that opened onto a low place in the line of dunes that fortressed them against the sea, against the edge of the world, against the wind that might blow chilly at the summer's end, if by then they hadn't been allowed to continue west, to settle in a city or a town, in a small house near a hospital, where he would work and Martha and Amira would walk each day to school, and Martha would befriend the other mothers and chat to them about the things that occupy women, and she would pretend interest in these things, and maybe she'd resume her work some day, her examination of the smallest parts of life, of molecules and all their spinning massless parts. And he was screaming for the young woman with the thin-framed glasses and the high forehead and the long blonde hair to go, to take care of her own business, to leave him in peace, he was tired and he needed to sleep, and he was off his bunk now and he had his hands on her arms and he was trying to make her rise from her seat and his arms suddenly were useless, they were pinned behind him somehow, and the young man was standing beside the young woman and they were looking down at him, down at the floor, and the woman had a hand over her mouth, and then her hands were twined together again, and they were moving up and down as though she were pleading, imploring, praying to God.

And so the storm came heaving down around him. The memory of it, as real and as violent as the thing itself. The young man and the woman stayed with him; he could feel the man's hands on his back and he could see through his fingers the woman's feet, the logo on her trainers, the mudsplatters on the sides of them, the greying laces.

Their slow retreat from the empty cabin and the clamped wheel and the monstrous box connected to it, the trafficker's terrible deceit. The complaining man saying, What fools we are, what fools we are, the tears carving lines along his fat cheeks, the swinging of the cabin door as they were knocked sideways by a violent list, the sudden acuteness of their angle to the sky, his thanks to God that they had hours of daylight left, that a ship might happen on them, a rescue ship, a navy boat, full of seasoned mariners who'd winch them to safety and bring them to land. The impossibility of making it back across the deck to the door of the hold, of hauling the door open, of remaining upright longer than a moment.

There was no reason to believe them to be dead. He pretended now, to please the woman with the glasses and the pale blotchy youth. It seemed important to them, this pretence. Were there other ships on patrol that day? Had other navies sent their people into the storm, having seen on their radar some other stricken craft? Of course. People paid less than he had paid to leave the coast – some people left in inflatable craft, dinghies, a bare step above a plaything, and foreign navy ships and rescue boats were on patrol day and night, balms to the consciences of governments.

He thought he should go to the tent and find the old man who had brought him food and water and clothes and apologize to him for attacking him, for squeezing his scrawny old neck, and then he'd hear the old man's words, Wives are easily found and daughters are easily made, and he'd shake and his breathing would become fast and ragged, like a man who'd just run a hundred metres at full speed, and he'd have to sit on his bunk and empty his mind and gather himself.

The woman came each day for a week with a notebook and she coaxed him and cajoled him and, after a few days, exhorted him, to tell her his story, and he began to speak and she made careful note of Martha's full name and of Amira's, and their dates of birth and their appearance and all the things that had happened in their town from the time that he saw the crucified boy until the day they left in the trafficker's jeep.

When will the boats be raised? he asked the young woman.

She said nothing for a while, just looked at him, and then she said, Some day, maybe, the boats will be raised. It's all they can do now to tend the stricken craft and take the living from the sea to safety. She said no more and the silence between them grew heavy, because he knew she had more to say and he could feel the weight of it, how she carried it heavily, this thing she was about to say. Your wife and your daughter, she began, and she stopped again and looked from his eyes to the floor, and she began again, with more resolve this time: Martha and Amira are not in this camp, or any other camp. You will not find them. Accept this, Farouk. And he said nothing back to her, but he asked if he could return to his tent, a new tent he'd been given with a single bunk and a tiny table and a cushion for a chair, and she said that he might.

He went to where the sand dunes were. To where he had thought the women and children would most likely be. He passed tents on the way to the dunes that had children in them, and men, and women sitting and standing and washing clothes and tending meals, and he lost his way a few times, and he read the letters and the numbers on the tents and he stepped through the straight ranks of canvas and tripped over guy ropes so often that a person watching would have thought him drunk, or an imbecile, and he reached the sand dunes and there was nothing on the far side but a fence, a thin barrier of wire stretched between wooden poles that leaned almost to falling in places, and gaps had been made in the fence along its length, and there was a shallow rocky drop from the far side of the wire to the beach, and there were no tents here, of course there weren't; there was no special quarantine or quarter for mothers and daughters separate from their husbands and fathers, and the beach was empty save for a man in corduroy trousers and a white shirt, and he was barefoot, and the man looked up at him, and he shook his head, and Farouk looked back at the man, and Farouk looked up from the water's edge at the man by the fence, and shook his head, and the man on the beach and the man at the fence fell to his knees and screamed, and his scream joined the wind that blew across the water from the east.

And late one evening he walked from the camp to the water's edge and he stood beneath the smirking moon and looked out across the sea, and he wondered at the stillness of it, as though its breath were held, as though it were too ashamed to reveal anything of itself to him, to admit to the violence latent in it, to the things it held, and he stripped himself naked and he walked out into it, and when he was a good way out, past, it seemed, the twin promontories that flanked the camp, the water still was only as far as his chest, and he lifted himself onto the surface of it and he struck out face-down for the empty horizon, and when he was sure he was far beyond his depth he flipped onto his back and looked at the long ragged tear of the galaxy, like a wound in the sky, weeping, and he exhaled and let his limbs fall still and he waited for the water to carry him down, and fill him, and slough his flesh and salt his guilty bones. But the water wouldn't take him. Each time he was immersed he came back up, and he tried and tried to drown; he opened his mouth to fill his lungs with water but he couldn't inhale it: his body pushed the flood back out. He kept himself perfectly still but the water buoyed him and held him at its surface and when his strength was gone and he could no longer resist it the current bore him gently back to shore.

A cyclone picked a woman up one time and carried her for many miles and dropped her at her former husband's door, unhurt. This miracle made them remember how they loved each other and they married again and had more children and lived happily ever after. An ever-after given by the wind. The sea could do the same then, surely. Carry a woman and a girl in a warm and gentle eddy for a thousand miles, along the edge of a continent, to a river-mouth, to a river, to a sun-warmed lake, and leave them on a pebble beach to rest until he found them there, and brought them home. He told that story to delegations from England, and Italy and Austria and France. Groups of officials sent to cherry-pick souls for their programmes, their projects, their exercises in mercy. He told them about the king and the beautiful girl he'd imprisoned and the slaughter of the songbirds, and they'd sit and gaze at him, and look at one another, and ask him to stop and for the number of his tent, and they'd take a copy of his camp identification and make a show of stapling it to his application and they'd thank him for his time. Some of them were angry with him, and asked him why he wasted their time. And in the end he found himself aboard a plane, and he was seated by the window looking down at the toe of Italy, and there was a family behind him spread along two rows of seats, of people from Aleppo, a mother and a father and two daughters and a son, who had walked to Turkey and sailed to Ios on a raft, and there was a family behind them from Urum al-Kubrah and they were chattering and laughing, and they had all looked sadly at Farouk when they had gathered at the delegation's office for their journey, and the men had sympathized with him, and one of them described how he had lost his brother and his parents in the fighting, and Farouk listened and returned the man's sympathy but he held his secret to himself, his sacred store of knowing, that Martha and Amira were alive, and were travelling on another tide.

Lampy

white Christmas! And he wheezed into the evening air, and his joke and his raspy laugh floated out from him in a yellowish cloud and vanished into the breeze. And it was a proud moment, a small becoming, being told a dirty joke directly like that, and being expected to get it, and to laugh.

Lampy could hear his grandfather now downstairs hawking and spitting into the range. He could just make out the sizzle of his phlegm. His stomach lurched a little at the sound. His mother didn't work on Fridays and he knew she'd be listening for him, looking out at the road now and again, watching for nobody, waiting for him to come down and eat the breakfast she'd made for him and left in the oven on a low heat in spite of Pop's protests that he should be told tough shit if he won't eat it like a normal Christian when it's made. Twenty-three years old, in the name of God, and still being babied. His mother would be twisting a tea-towel in her hands, back and forth, as though trying to wring some peace from it, some way of settling herself. He could hear her downstairs, moving around the kitchen and the front room, busy always, moving always, talking to herself in a way that would seem strange to any-one not used to hearing her; laughing here and there at some recollection, some good story she'd been told and had kept for herself, for the times she was without company. It sometimes seemed to him that his mother lived in a world of ghosts and angels: they swirled and flocked about her all the time. She read book after book, about angels, and about awareness and mindfulness and the afterlife, and she saw signs everywhere: in magpies' numbers and robins' stares and chickens' wishbones and the sudden appearance of feathers, tiny and white; all these things were messages from angels, or from her mother who was dead a few years before Lampy was born, and had to be mulled over and deciphered. She'd address them directly sometimes, and she'd still herself to receive their answers, her head angled to one side, her eyes filled with light, and she'd nod her thanks after a few moments, and go on about her business with a smile.

His mother asked him questions now and then, but never seemed to hear him when he answered. As though she knew already all his truths. She never lost her patience with him, and sometimes still she put her hand on his face, out of the blue, when he was just sitting there at the table, and she looked at him with something unknowable in her eyes, some distant thing, and she'd run her fingers through his hair, and he felt embarrassed when she did it, and uncomfortable, but still and all he'd hate it if she stopped. She'd stood beside him the morning of the Leaving Cert results and read them from the sheet in his hand. He'd gone to the school early, to get it over and done with. That way he'd avoid the lads, and have to show no one his marks. Only the swots were there for nine. She'd nodded and smiled and kissed his cheek. You did very well, so you did. And she moved away across the kitchen floor and lined the ware up to be washed and whispered to the empty air, He did, so he did. Very well. English Higher B1. The rest are all Cs. Not enough points for any of his choices. What about it? He's only young.

He knew the rhythms of the house and the two people below him, the syncopated beats of them, the tides that flowed and ebbed with no regularity but with a strange and comforting predictability, according to his grandfather's form, his aches and moods and petty defeats and tiny triumphs, his mother's movements back and forward from the present to the past. Friday mornings were always the same. Pop would have a feast of stories from the pub the night before. He could hear his grandfather telling a story now.

So I says I to him, do you know something, you're the cut head off of that actor fella, what's this his name is, oh, ya, that's it . . . George Clooney. And he nearly shat himself he was so happy. And once everyone was finished congratulating him on the compliment he was after getting and admiring him and agreeing away with me and it was all gone grand and quiet again, I says, I says, Oh, hold on, no, it was the other lad I meant, sounds nearly the same, what's it again, oh, ya . . . and I waited a minute till every fucker along the bar was cocking an ear, and I says, I says . . . Mickey Rooney! And I'd say he nearly burst his gut trying to frustrate his desire to fuckin kill me. And I raising my glass to him and toasting his health and all. You should of seen the puss on him. That showed the cunt and his new coat.

And Lampy smiled and he could hear his mother saying, *Dad*, in pretended offence at the terrible word, and his grandfather laughing and wheezing and hawking again, and he could hear the range door opening, and a spit and a sizzle, and the range door closing and his mother complaining about the spitting and he knew his grandfather had only been practising the story, that he, Lampy, was the intended audience, and the feeling this knowledge gave him was not quite articulable, this strange thrill of pride. His grandfather was wicked; when he was in form his tongue could slice the world in two.

Where's Lampy, anyway? Admiring himself above in the mirror. He'll have it wore out looking into it. Once he's not pulling himself. DAD! His mother sounded cross now, but his grandfather was in his stride, talking on and on. And there was another lad there telling all and sundry about how he was going to a fancy-dress party inside in City Hall in aid of some crowd does be helping the refugees or the panda bears or something and he was wondering to know what should he go as and I says to him, I says, Do you know now what you should do? And he knew well there was something coming and he let on not to hear me at all, and so I says again, louder, Hye, hye, do you know now what you should do? And I could see the whole place again was waiting for the punchline, and Podge even stopped pulling a pint halfway and he was smiling to himself, he knew so he did, and there was a few tough chaws from the Island Field in and they were waiting for it, and I says to him, Do you know what you should do? And it killed him to say it, but he had to, he had no choice, and he says, What? And a face of murder on him, and I says, real even and slow and serious . . . You should put on your own clothes and go as a prick! And the whole place was in stitches, there was fuckin pandemonium, and he was fit to fuckin split me open.

And Lampy checked the snow again and hoped it wasn't sticking, that the ground was wet and not icy, because he was driving the new bus, and he wasn't too confident in it: it was wider than the old one, and worth a lot more, and the Grogans from the home were up in a heap about it and the cost of it, even though it was three years old and an import, and the fuckers of inspectors who had declared the old one unfit for purpose. He put on two pairs of socks and his new eight-hole Docs that his cousin Shane said were twenty years out of fashion but he didn't care because they gave him an extra half-inch of height, and he buckled his jeans and he stood in front of the mirror and flexed his biceps and tried to get his hair to sit right and he wondered was his T-shirt too tight and he decided it wasn't, and he wondered how far

Eleanor would let him go that night and he wondered should he take her somewhere besides Supervalu car park and he hoped the Civic wouldn't let him down again, she'd break it off for sure, and he hoped his mother wouldn't try to make him have toast because he'd have to tell her again how he was off carbs and Pop would go to town on him and pretend to be up in arms over him refusing to eat toast and call him a queer and a nancy boy and every sort of a name.

And he felt good, and he smiled as he went downstairs, in anticipation of the stories, which would be embellished in repetition, drawn to the last. He felt he might get through the day without being winded, smacked in the stomach by some unbidden memory or thought or worry or regret. He might be able to go to the home and do his work and get his cash from James Grogan and drive to the city and pick up the young one and chat for a minute or two with her old man about the scores from the day and how Liverpool were shite again this season and he might be able to talk to her without calling her the wrong name and pissing her off, and they might make plans to go on a holiday in the summer and he might be normal, he might be a lad like any other lad, doing normal things, holding himself straight, holding his temper.

He knew that Pop had heard him on the stairs. Here he's on, he was saying, and he was clearing his throat again, in preparation, Lampy knew, for the retelling of the stories he had just practised on his daughter. Lampy toyed for a moment with the idea of cutting his grandfather off, saying, I heard you already, Pop, George Clooney, Mickey Rooney, fancy dress, blah blah blah. But he couldn't do it, he couldn't put the boot in like that. Or maybe he could. It depended what way his grandfather greeted him. If he called him a queer or accused him of pulling himself all morning above in the bathroom he would listen to no stories. He'd wrap his sausages and rashers in a slice of brown bread – fuck the carbs – and he'd squirt some ketchup on them, and he'd go, and Pop could tell his stories to the dog.

The other night his mother had lit a Christmas candle. Pop had moaned about it coming sooner every year and Lord Almighty they weren't even out of November, and she'd told him to mind his own business. The candle was fat and tall and she'd bared the bay window of curtains and blinds so she could set it in the centre of the sill. To bless his journeys, to light his way home. She hated him driving, he knew. She cried at every news report of fatal accidents; she blessed herself and whispered prayers for mercy for their souls, for their poor families, their poor families. Lord, can you imagine it? Could you not leave the car? she'd say, every time he looked for his keys. She'd never help him find them. Would you not let Pop drop you off to wherever you're going? And he'd feel himself getting cross with her and he wouldn't answer her and he'd swear beneath his breath as he searched under newspapers and behind cushions and along the mantelpiece and worktops and shelves. And Pop would say, Will you leave the boy alone, there's fear of him, he's no fool. He won't act the ape on the road. And he'd see Pop looking at him, with a funny expression on his face, worry, and something else, a kind of resignation, and he wondered then if Pop knew somehow, about the times he drove full pelt along the narrow road from Lackanavea, his eyes full of tears, his seatbelt off, the twin piers of the railway bridge approaching fast, thinking, One flick of my wrist, one flick. That'd show her.

The first conversation he'd ever had with Chloe was about the three little pigs. On the night bus coming back from town. He'd spotted her in the Chicken Hut and she'd smiled at him and he'd nodded, trying to be cool, and she'd laughed at him and looked away. Then on the bus she'd asked his friend Dave if he minded swapping seats and Dave said, No bother but I just farted, and Lampy felt like killing him but she just smiled and took Dave's seat and she said nothing until the bus started moving and neither did he, and then she turned to him and said, You know the story of the three little pigs, who were fucked off by their mother because she was sick of their shit? And all he could do was nod, and watch the dimple that creased the skin along her cheek, but only on one side, and the light that flashed in her blue-green eyes, and the way her eyebrows arced as she spoke, the way she whispered, her smile, her bad smile, the redness of her lips, the perfect shape of them, the way she leaned close to him, like she was telling him a terrible secret, something filthy and delicious. You know how there are two versions? One where the big bad wolf blows the first two fucking idiots' houses down because they're made from twigs and straw but they escape and run to the smart pig's house because it's made from blocks and the big bad wolf busts his gut trying to blow down the concrete house and in the end the little fat fuckers coax him down the chimney and boil him alive? And the one where the wolf blows down the fucking idiot brothers' houses and eats the fuckers? I way prefer that version. And not the version of that version where the smart fucker, before he boils the wolf alive, manages some-how to rescue the idiots from the wolf's belly. That's bullshit. They need to be fucking dead. They deserve it. Don't they? And Lampy nodded, though he had no idea what she was on about, she was clearly pissed, but he had a pain in his crotch and in his heart, and he knew he was in love.

He only bought the Honda to please her. She loved going for spins. She'd lie right back in the passenger seat and turn the stereo up full and close her eyes and tell him to just drive and he'd have to force himself to keep his eyes on the road and not on her legs, on the place where her skirt rode up along her thigh, and his head would spin a little sometimes. Once she asked him to drive towards Ballina; she said she'd heard there was a place you could drive to, the very top of a mountain, where you could see five counties on a clear day, up past the graves of some fuckers from the old days? And when they got there she took a condom from her handbag and told him to put it on, all the while holding his eye, and she took off her underwear and lay back and said, Come on, Lampy, and it was all over in seconds and she laughed at him and they did it again a few minutes later and she said it was much better, and it was, and he'd thought as he drove back down the snaking mountain road that nothing mattered now but this, that this was the day all his days had been for.

He was stopped on the stairs now, halfway down, and the knuckles of his left hand were white from the force of his grip on the banister. The thought of Chloe always stopped him, paralysed him. Her slender hands and blue-green eyes, her soft laugh and gentle shrug to stop him in his tracks, the pain she'd leave him in, the pain she left him in, terminal it seemed to him. He'd surely die of it. Eleanor was small and dark-haired and she smiled a lot and she had lovely big eyes and massive tits in fairness, and there was something very sexy about the uniform she wore for work in Brown Thomas, but he knew that deep down she knew she was just a handy shift, a rebounder, that he was still in love with someone else, but she'd stick around in hope another while.

Chloe was different: angular, firm; the memory of the arch of her back and the press of her ribs against her skin scalded him. Even her lips seemed hard against his, urgent, as though it were her kissing him, as though he had no choice. Eleanor was soft in contrast, warm, eager to please him; her lips were full and sweet-tasting. Chloe was going to end up in a big house, he knew, with a high wall around it and remote-control gates. Eleanor would end up wherever; she'd be happy and she'd have loads of kids and she'd be really nice to them. She'd be forgiving. He wondered should he marry her and be done with it. He could love her if he really tried.

He reckoned she'd see how the Christmas went, if he'd stop calling her the wrong name, if he'd get her a decent present. Eleanor was from the city; he only met her twice a week or so. She didn't know the full extent of it, the way he'd watch out for flashes of Chloe here and there, waiting for a downturned smile of pity and a tiny wave, a gentle push in the chest in the chipper when he tried to talk to her but all his sentences were drowned.

He thought about their spot, their mountaintop, up past the Graves of the Leinstermen where they'd sat after doing it for the last time, and he'd held her hand, stroking the back of it with his thumb, wondering at the feeling of the narrow bones beneath her skin, not knowing what was in store for him, what was coming. How fragile they'd felt to him, how perfect; he wished that he could see them for a second, see her from the inside out, inhabit her, possess her completely. He loved her so much, that was all, he loved her. She asked him could they drive into Limerick as far as McDonald's. He still couldn't figure out why she did that, why she chose Micky D's car park to rip his heart out. Had she planned on eating first? Micky D's was fucking ruined for him now. It's not working with me being in college in Dublin, she said. It's not fair on you. We'll still be friends, always.

And he said nothing to her for a long while because he couldn't trust his voice. There was a lump in his throat, an actual lump, and it was blocking his windpipe, it seemed, because he was having trouble breathing properly; his heart was beating hard and irregular in his chest and the colour was gone from the front of McDonald's, the yellow M was grey and the lights shone white and every car in the car park was black, and he closed his eyes tight and when he opened them again the world was in colour and he caught a hold of himself and he said, I'll move to Dublin. I'm doing fuck-all else. I could get a job up there. I should be up there with you anyway, the amount of freaks there are in that place. You shouldn't be walking round alone. And she smiled and bit her bottom lip and put her hand on his and said, Oh, Lampy, you're a lovely guy, you really are. I'm well able to look after myself. I'm sorry, Lampy. Will you bring me home? And he asked her why she'd asked him to bring her the whole way to Limerick to McDonald's if she just wanted to go home again and she said she wasn't hungry any more, she didn't think she'd be this sad, and that hurt him more, that idea of her being surprised that she was so sad. He bent across to kiss her and she turned her face so he got her cheek, and his temper rose then suddenly, and he put his hand on her tit and squeezed hard and she screeched and punched him on the bottom of his chin and she said, FUCK, what the FUCK, Lampy? and she was wringing her hand in pain, and he was telling her to get the fuck out of his car, she was only a gowl, and she sat straight up in her seat, crying silently, saying, low, in a whisper, Bring me home, Lampy, just bring me fucking home.

He'd only seen her once since then, after the nightclub, four or five months ago. She wouldn't talk to him. Her brothers stood between them in the chipper, blocking him, saying, Come on, Lamp, don't be stupid, we don't want to fall out with you. And he took a swing at the eldest lad and missed, and he slipped on a ketchup sachet someone had opened and dropped, and he'd hopped off the floor of the chipper and the whole place laughed at him, and he saw from the ground that Chloe was standing near him and she was looking straight ahead and she had her hand to her face and her friend had her arm around her, as though to protect her, and he was saying, Chloe, please, just come outside with me a minute, and her brothers were lifting him off the floor now and saying, Go on to fuck, Lampy, leave it, man, leave it, and the small little dark lad from the chipper was out from behind the counter and he was saying something in a high-pitched voice and Lampy couldn't make it out so he swung again and missed again and the chipper lad had him in a chokehold and he was out through the door and into the street and he was falling, falling.

One of the Curran boys was in her year in Trinity. He

didn't know which one: they were identical and they were both cunts. He told him she was going with a Dublin lad. He was tall, he played rugby. His father was a barrister. That's all he knew.

He thought of the day Pop rang her mother. What possessed him? Oh, Pop. What the fuck did you do? Pop standing in the hallway by the phone table, bow-legged, the way he always stood, his feet wide apart like a drunk man about to scrap, his face red and his white hair lifting from his scalp as though in indignation. It took a while for it to register with Lampy what was going on. He'd been crying in his room just like a child. Pop's voice, loud and cracking, saying, Ye fuckers never thought anything of him anyway, ye think ye're big-shots, and that's the God's honest truth, ye think ye're too good for the likes of us, ye think that little strap of a one was too good for my boy, and she only a strap, that lady, a half-reared little rap, well, she better stay away from my boy, that's all I'll say. And the voice of Chloe's mother, soft and placatory, and he couldn't quite make out her words but she was saying something like I know you're upset and you don't mean that, Mr Shanley, and we really have to let them live their own lives, they'll have their hearts broken a fair few times each before they're twice married, won't they? And she was laughing softly, and Pop was huffing fuming breaths out through his nose, and he was opening his mouth again to speak, and Lampy was taking the stairs in fours, and diving for the phone, and pushing down the contacts, and nearly knocking Pop down on the floor, and he was pushing Pop and shouting, WHAT THE FUCK, POP, WHAT THE FUCKING FUCK? And Pop was on his back foot, wordless now, embarrassed suddenly, and Lampy nearly hit him but he caught himself in time, and instead he said, I'm

He was plagued, these days. He didn't know why. He couldn't still his mind. That was why he kept it going with Eleanor: she talked on and on about X *Factor* and *I'm A Celebrity* and all sorts of shite and she was pretty and she was game enough but he had to coax her a bit and that was fine, it helped, it soothed him, his soft advances and her fake demurrals, her ceaseless voice and her lilting city accent, her sweet teasing, her expert tongue. He played and replayed incidents, over and over, times he should have held his fire with Pop, with his mother, with Chloe. He couldn't keep a lid on his foul temper. He wondered was his father just as bad. He thought a lot about the last day he'd played hurling, the day he fucked up in defence and they nearly lost the Junior A semi-final because of him, and Tony Delahunty asked him coming off was he stupid, and something snapped in his head and he said, Don't call me stupid, Tony, don't call me stupid now again, and Tony Delahunty laughed at him and said, Or what? And Lampy said nothing but he squared up a bit and Tony Delahunty told him sit down to fuck and Lampy knocked shoulders with him passing from the sideline to the bench and said, Bollix, loud enough for him to hear, and Cian Delahunty stood up from the subs' bench and said, Don't get smart, Lamp, don't fuckin shoulder my oul fella like that again, and I heard what you called him, and Lampy said, You're a bollix too, like father like son, and

Cian Delahunty said, A lot you'd know about fathers, at least
I know who *my* father *is*, and Lampy opened the skin above
Cian Delahunty's eye with a head-butt and the rest of the subs
got between them and the ref came over wanting to know
what in the fuck was going on and threatening to call off the
match and hand it to the Cormacs, and Pop was over from
the stand and he was saying, Come on, son, come on to fuck,
don't mind this shower of useless cunts, they wouldn't hurl
their way out of a wet paper bag, and there was nothing said
on the way home but he wondered how much of it Pop had
heard, how much Pop knew, about anything.

He'd asked him once. Straight out. He was ten or maybe
eleven. Where's my father, Pop? And Pop had kept on marking
out his cuts on the workshop counter and his lips were moving
in silent calculation, and after a little while Pop said, What's
that, son? though Lampy knew he'd heard him. Where's my
father? And Pop kept marking his cuts with his stubby pencil
and his twelve-inch ruler and he repeated Lampy's question
under his breath, as though he were trying to remember or to
figure out what the words meant, and he didn't look at Lampy,
but he answered. Beyond in England somewhere, as far as I
know. What's his name? I don't know. How don't you know?
How don't I? Because I was never told. Nor did I ask. If a
person wants you to know something they'll tell you. Do you
know anything about him? Divil a bit that was ever known
except that your mother fell for him when she was young and
they had a fling and when he found out she was expecting he
fecked off. Like many a man along the years. He didn't want
the hassle of it, I suppose. Some men just aren't fatherly, son. It
was nothing against you, anyway. I never laid eyes on the man,
nor was I ever told his name. I have a feeling he was from the

city. That's all I was ever told about it and now you know as much as me. And Lampy understood that he would be given no more, even if Pop had more to give.

When he was small he hadn't known there was a difference. Mam was Mam and Pop was Pop. Husband and wife and mother and father and grandfather and son and daughter and grandson were all just words, and the only words that were ever made flesh were Mam and Pop. Then someone told him the meaning of the word bastard. At lunchtime in the yard when he was in fourth class. A lad from sixth class. He walked up to where Lampy was eating his sandwiches, sitting on the low grass bank at the top of the yard, and said, You're a bastard. And there were a few behind him grinning and the first lad was eating a bag of crisps and he was looking at Lampy, chewing his crisps, smiling, waiting for Lampy's reaction, and all Lampy could say was, What? You're a bastard, the lad said again, and he finished his crisps and he crumpled the bag and put it in his trouser pocket. Do you know what a bastard is? And Lampy didn't answer, so the boy explained: A bastard is a person with no father. So I'm not swearing if I call you a bastard. I'm just telling a fact. And Lampy could tell that the boys either side of him had stopped eating and stopped moving and were waiting for him to react, and he felt a kind of lightness in his middle, and a weird feeling in his crotch, like someone had grabbed his balls and was holding them tight, and the explainer of the word bastard was licking his fingers one by one, up as far as the second knuckle, and he was narrow and tall and he was looking at Lampy while he sucked and licked his long thin fingers, and Lampy knew he was one of the Pratts, his father had an office downtown that said PRATT over it and a few other things that Lampy didn't understand,

and someone was saying, Oooh, wouldn't take that, wouldn't take that, and Brother Rutledge was meant to be supervising the yard but he was at the far end, down by the sixth-class bike shed, and his back was turned, and Lampy heard Pop's voice saying, Do your best to stay out of fights, son, but if you ever have to throw a dig, aim for the Adam's apple. Like this, look. And Pop made a weapon of his hand by curling his fingers so his knuckles jabbed forward. And don't tuck in your thumb, you could break it. Push it in against the side of your index finger. And keep your eye on the fucker's Adam's apple and jab straight and hard. And Pop had shown him over and over again what to do, and Mam had come in and caught them at it, jabbing and feinting around the kitchen, laughing and shouting, and she'd given out to them and told them to stop, and Pop had reminded him once more: Adam's apple. Look, that bobbly yoke there in the throat. And he'd formed his left hand into a blade of knuckles again and winked. And Lampy pushed his left foot into the bank now and sprang upwards and the Pratt boy was sucking the salt from the fingers of his right hand and Lampy could see that he had a sharp and bobbly Adam's apple and it was working up and down with the sucking of the salt, and he connected hard and clean, and the bold explainer of bastard fell backwards against his little gang and onto the ground and he was making a weird thin ragged sound and his two hands of licked fingers were at his throat and his face was bright red and his eyes were bulging and the lads were all up and in a ring and shouting, ROW, ROW, ROW, and Brother Rutledge was running in his black smock towards them and Lampy felt his friends' hands clapping against his back and they were saying, Aboy, Lamp, aboy, Lamp, you got him, and Lampy was bothered for the first time that day, and aware of the differences between people, and he was bothered and aware ever since.

He heard a man ask his grandfather who he was at a hurling match one time. A few years after he'd punched Niall Pratt in the throat. Under twelve or under fourteen, he couldn't remember. He'd played badly. That's a boy of yours, is it, that was brought off? Number seven? And his grandfather told the man he was, yes, that was his boy. The man looked away and smirked and looked back again and opened his mouth to speak and Pop drew himself from his hunch and he balled his fists and said, Have you more to say? Have you more to say about it? And the man stepped back and checked the sky and then the ground but couldn't find a better answer and so he just said, no, he was only asking, that was all. And Pop noticed him then, he'd been sitting just behind him all along, and he said, Come here, son, and sit beside me. Don't mind them bollixes at all. Bringing off their best player and he not even warmed up.

And as he reached the bottom of the stairs the sudden unbidden memory caused in Lampy a familiar prickle, a ghostly breath of guilt or shame, or some other thing, some other kind of feeling with no name, not one that he knew anyway. Another memory came to him, just as he reached the kitchen door, and it stopped him, like a hand pressed firmly on his chest, like a bouncer at a nightclub door inside in town, one of the places where they let on to be members only, the Icon or somewhere. Stall on there, boy. Have you ID? No, I must have left it in your mother's house. He couldn't time these memories, these stupid things that made him stop sometimes and stand with his hand to his forehead and his eyes closed, that paralysed him. Pop waiting for him to walk him home after training. Him ducking past the hurling-field gate where Pop was standing smoking a fag, walking fast along the inside of the wall and through Kelly's back gate to avoid him. Pop arriving in and not mentioning that he'd been waiting. The thought of Pop waiting, watching in the gate towards the changing-room door. Going in after a while to see was he there, asking Tony Delahunty where he was, Tony saying he's gone a small while, Dixie. Pop saying, Oh, feck, right, I must have just missed him.

James Grogan asked him weeks ago to supervise the day room at the home. Up to then he'd tipped around, cleaning rooms and changing sheets and driving the bus when needed. On his own, sometimes, though he knew there was meant to be a nurse on the bus when certain residents were being transported to and from appointments and home visits. The Grogans were chancers. They'd swindle the devil, Pop said. All you need do is sit and watch them, Lampy, James Grogan said. Make sure that no one wanders or chokes or falls out of their chair. If anything happens you run for the nurse or one of the women. You needn't be a hero at all. I'm offering to pay you to sit on your arse. Will you do it? And Lampy said he would, though he'd heard a woman had died in that day room a few years ago, right there in front of the picture window, in her own husband's arms, and that it had happened all of a shot: she'd gotten up from her seat and sat into her husband's lap and died. And the husband had followed her a few weeks later, just closed his eyes one day and slipped away. So it was a bigger thing by far than James Grogan made it out to be. But still he was glad. He liked the day room, the peace of it, the circle of people, some of them doting, some of them as sharp as tacks. There was a woman who knitted scarf after scarf, her hands going like pistons, and she never once looked down at her needles or her wool, but looked all around her all day long and talked about the others to Lampy. Look at this one, she'd say, she's deaf as a stone, you know, and this one, gone fat as a fool, and your man across and his breeches on back to front, Lord, what a shop of crocks, and she'd shake her head and her hands would piston on, and Lampy came to like the soft cackle of her, the wickedness that shone behind her glasses. You're a fine-looking boy, she said one day. You've a fierce big forehead, though. You must have plenty brains. How is it you're doing this job?

And a man one day last week had called him Declan. Declan, have you my car keys? Declan. Declan. Will you find my car keys for me until we go home? May will have our dinner made. Declan. And when Lampy went to him to settle him a bit the man took hold of his hand and his grip was strong and tight, and he was saying, Good lad, Declan, you're a great lad, have you the keys found? And Lampy said, I'm not Declan, and the old man looked confusedly at him for a long moment, and then was silent, and he said, Oh, yes. I get mixed up. I do. I get my wires crossed all the time, these days. And when Lampy looked across at the man a while later he saw that his eyes were closed and his lips were moving and there were tears on his cheeks. The knitter looked at Lampy and nodded at the crying man and rolled her eyes to Heaven and back and said, Poor misfortune. That Declan he's looking for is gone a long time now, God help us. Abroad somewhere, like my own lad. And then she looked back at Lampy and she studied him a while and said, What's in the past can't be changed and what's to come can't be known and you can't give your life to worrying. Sure you can't. All you have to do is be kind and you'll have lived a good life. And Lampy agreed with her and she chuckled softly and resumed her inspections of her comrades.

And in the kitchen Pop was laughing still, and coughing still, and Lampy's mother was putting on toast, and he decided he'd just eat it: there was no point going through the rigmarole. Pop was doing his surprised act, the most annoying part of his repertoire. Oh, begod, look out. Look what's after appearing. The dead arose and appeared to many. Lazarus, Lazarus, up from his pit. Lord, you've a great job. What time are you left stroll in at? Any oul time at all? Well for you. And Lampy said, I'm only doing a bus run today. And Pop said, You are. Just that: You are. And the way he said it was maddening, the suggestion in his voice, the intimation that Lampy was lying, that he was meant to be at work all day but had just felt like sleeping in; it was enough to make Lampy want to scream at him, to catch him by the collar and shake him, but he never would. I've only to drive a few of them into town to their therapy places and drop a couple to their children's houses, Pop, he said, and I'm getting fifty quid for it, and he hoped Pop would leave it there, just leave it. But he didn't. You are, he said. And Lampy slammed his hand so hard on the table that his plate hopped and his mother jerked her head towards him and her eyes were wide with surprise and Lampy shouted, I FUCKING AM! And he wondered why he couldn't keep his cool, why he let the old man dig beneath his skin.

And his grandfather sat and sulked in near silence, only muttering beneath his breath that all he said was that he was and what was wrong with that? He was, wasn't he? And he didn't try to tell Lampy any of his stories, about George Clooney or Mickey Rooney or pricks going to fancy-dress parties or anything else, and Lampy could feel the air around him thickening with his own imposturous anger, with his grandfather's temper and disappointment, with his mother's

he was telling someone whom he couldn't see that this was normal, that the river was tidal as far as Curragower, that it was just a fast tide coming in, not to worry, and the bridge groaned and shook and collapsed into the water and the water was warm around him, and it carried him upstream past King's Island and over the salmon weirs, and the river rushed inland against itself, away from the sea, and he was laughing when he woke, and as the dream faded he thought how easy it would be to let himself be carried to his end. To close his eyes and fall.

James Grogan met him at the door. Come on, you're late, he said, and Lampy checked his watch. You told me be here at twelve. I'm a minute early. Oh, are you? Well, excuse me, wait there till I get you a trophy, or is it a minute's fucking overtime you want? And Lampy left it there. There was no point back-answering the prick. Okay, James Grogan said, okay now. Right. Listen. And James Grogan went through the list of drop-offs and pick-ups, and Lampy didn't need to listen too closely because it was the same every week, he knew the list of people and places by heart by now, and he watched James Grogan's fat jaw working up and down, and the tiny white crescents of gunk at the sides of his mouth, like manky little brackets for his words, and he wondered how the grisly fat fuck's wife let him ride her and she a fine thing, all tanned and blonde and vicious curves, and she was up over forty but she was in serious nick and Lampy felt himself harden and he panicked and made himself think about the injection you have to get into the inside of your knob if you get chlamydia, the tiny spikes that umbrella from the top of the needle when it's in there, and the doctor has to pull it out hard, and his horn damped, like it always did when he used that trick, and he was glad of that trick, he'd used it many times in places where a man can't be striking horns indiscriminately, Mass, places like that, not that he went too much, but he'd gotten a horn at a funeral once, a friend of Pop's, kneeling down looking at the arse of the woman in front of him, the hint of red lace at the top of her black skirt, the faint outline of her knickers, the little zip on her skirt, and when he'd sat back up he'd had to lean forward because he'd had no jumper or jacket or anything to put over his lap and he had solid wood and all he could hear was Pop's cross whisper: What the fuck is wrong with you? Are you sick? Sit up straight, will you?

Pop always made out that the Grogans had only got permission to build the home in that beautiful green field because of brown envelopes flying about the place inside in town. How is it, Pop often asked, that Bridie Dwyer below in Ballygash wasn't able to get permission to put a couple of rows of blocks on top of her front wall and a high solid gate so herself and the mad prick she's married to could run around their garden in the nip? Ha-ha-ha! And Lampy would laugh and his mother would tut-tut and shake her head, and Pop, having caught his breath and cleared his throat in a monarchical fashion, would be spurred on to greater explicitness. They're a pair of nudies, you know! Notorious, they are! Isn't that what you call them, Florence? Nudies? Nudists, Dad, Lampy's mother would say, and her correction would go unheeded. And anyway they're not. Oh, begod they are, a pair of nudie-nawdies! Yerra go way, Lampy, you must have heard that. That just proves now once and for all that you do be going around the place like a gom, looking down out of your mouth at your shoes going in and out before you. The world and his nephew knows them two are a pair of nudie-nawdies. She runs around in her birthday suit any day the weather allows and Murty tears around behind her with his lad in his hand! There was many a car written off at that bad bend outside their house, with people's eyes stole by Bridie's diddies flapping up and down or Murty's oul balls flying about the place. And Lampy would laugh so much his head would reel and his eyes would stream.

And Lampy realized suddenly that James Grogan had stopped talking to him and was talking to one of the nurses who'd appeared beside him, a small round foreign lady who always seemed sad, and she was saying, It's ridiculous, it's ridiculous, and James Grogan was saying, Don't worry about it, just do your own job and let others do theirs, and the foreign nurse, whose name he couldn't think of though he knew it sounded Irish, Mary or Marie or Maria or something like that, walked away shaking her head, and Patsy Fox the handyman had brought the bus, all loaded up with oldies, around from the day-room door, and Patsy was getting out and he was winking at him and smirking behind James Grogan's back and James Grogan was saying, Okay, Lampy, is that all clear? And Lampy said it was, no bother, sound out.

The snow had stopped and all the clouds had cleared and the pale gibbous moon looked wrong against the morning blue, like it wasn't meant to be there, like a lad wandering home after a whole night on the beer, washed-out and dying sick. The temperature reading on the dash was zero. There was some kind of rambling chatter going on at the back of the bus and Mr Collins was near the front, leaning out from his seat, telling him about the time he'd been a bus driver in London. All the streets and roads he'd driven every day. All the routes he knew, and he wondered would he know them still. If he had a chance to go there ever again. Maybe he should have stayed beyond. He drove a bus here too, you know, for CIÉ. Until he retired. A gentler occupation this side of the water by far. Not as many darkies or thugs. We've our fair share all the same, though. And the woman next to Mr Collins shushed him and Mr Collins talked on regardless. And he was telling Lampy for the seventh or eighth time the one about when he was held up in Bethnal Green, how the fella held the cold blade to his face and made off with the cashbox but not his wallet; that was the time before there was a divide between the drivers and passengers, you know, and that was when he decided to come home and he was let combine his service in both places for the purposes of his pension, thank God, because only for that he'd be out on his ear, and did Lampy know bus drivers were paid less than bin-men in those days in London, but still all the same he wouldn't change anything, not even the time he was held up, because that experience stood to him in later life, it galvanized him sort of, and Mr Collins was talking on and on but Lampy couldn't hear him any more, and the reading on the speedometer rose by five and the reading on the outside temperature gauge dropped by one.

The road slopes down from Coolderry, winding and narrow, lined with sycamore trees. It was coated with fallen leaves turned to mush and hardened again by the frost. Lampy's knuckles were whitening on the steering wheel. The road forks at the bottom of the slope and just before it, fifty yards from Con Kelleher's house, the big Mercedes that Lampy's employers were in hock up to their ear-holes for shimmied left and right, sending Lampy's heart into a hammering spasm of ragged beats and thumping palpitations. He couldn't think of a thing to do so he didn't think at all, but his hands decided by themselves to hold fast to the wheel and his foot took it upon itself to ease off the throttle and gently onto the brake and as the bus slid past Con Kelleher's high gate the traction control reined in the slide and the wayward tyres regained their grip on the cold road and the anti-lock brakes slowed the wagon to a gentle speed and the cheeks of Lampy's bony arse unclenched themselves as his heart settled back into its normal, sinus rhythm.

And Mr Collins was saying, Oh, japers, japers cripes, you held her well, lad, begodden you did, and a shriller voice behind him was saying, Hey, hey, you driving, you with the big ears, are you trying to do away with us or what? And the dash suddenly lit, all the lights came on at once, for the battery and the oil and the ABS and the overheat warning and the handbrake warning and the seatbelt warning and the airbag warning, and a message was flashing in yellow, ECU ERROR, and then LIMP HOME MODE and the new Mercedes mini-bus, which had nearly killed James Grogan to buy, coughed softly and slowed itself to the pace of a brisk walk.

What's going on? Hey, Big Ears, what's going on? Come on in the name of God or we'll miss our hydrotherapy. I better not miss my hydrotherapy over your fooling. And Mr Collins turned to his comrade and told him to be quiet, to shut up in the name of God, it was hardly the boy's fault there was something gone wrong with the bus. You couldn't trust these modern yokes. Too many faldidles and fiddly bits. Microchips. Whatever the blazes they are. Yokes designed to go wrong. Give me a Bedford 240 any day. An engine and wheels and a seat. What more could you need? And someone else was saying, I'll need to go to the toilet soon, and someone else was saying, Ah, now, he hasn't big ears at all, but he has a fine size of a head, he has the biggest head I've ever seen anyway, and that's for sure, and someone else was saying, Margaret, Margaret, will you go out as far as the slatted house and see did I leave my stick inside the door of it?

Mr Collins was up from his seat and standing crooked at his elbow now and he was squinting at the instruments, and he was reading the message there slowly, loudly: Limp . . . home . . . mode, it says. Begod we'll be a fair old while limping home at this rate, you're as well off park her up to Hell. And Lampy could hear a hubbub behind him of grainy voices Chinese-whispering Mr Collins's words: Limp home mode, what's that? Limp home mode, the yoke says. Who has to limp home? I'm limping nowhere only in as far as the pool. Hye, Bighead, who has to limp home? And some of them were laughing, and someone, Mrs Coyne, he was fairly sure, was saying, Ah, whisht now, don't be tormenting the boy, he has enough on his plate without you giving off and carrying on like bold children. And Mr Collins was saying, Go easy, now, lad, take her handy, watch the temperature gauge for fear she'd be overheating, you could blow the head gasket very easy, handy now, handy.

The heater was still working, thank God, but he turned it down because beads of sweat had started to form along his forehead. He felt embarrassed, and he wasn't sure why. He knew he should be turning around and saying something to the oldies, telling them it was grand, they'd get there, not to be worrying, but he couldn't get the words straight in his head. The throttle wouldn't respond at all, except when he lifted off: the bus would slow then to a crawl. Con Kelleher's yard was a small bit back along the road. Con wouldn't be there at this time on a Friday but Lampy knew he could swing around at the old creamery and leave the bus back at Con's and he could ring Mickey Briars to tear up to the home and get the old bus and bring it down here to him and he could transfer the oldies quick enough, he thought, there was no bad cases on the bus, and they could, all going well, be back on the road within twenty minutes, if Mickey didn't act the prick.

He reached into his pocket for his phone and someone said, Oh, begod, look out, he has the phone out, and Mr Collins was saying, Be careful now you don't meet a squad, they'll pull you for that as quick as look at you, and Lampy suppressed a savage urge to scream, SHUT THE FUCK UP at him, JUST SHUT THE FUCK UP, WILL YOU, and Mickey Briars's phone was ringing and ringing and ringing and Mickey wasn't answering and Lampy wondered what in the name of

God he could be doing to say he couldn't answer his phone, and Lampy imagined Mickey holding his ringing phone out from himself and squinting down at it and seeing his name on the screen and taking his time answering out of some sort of spite, or cuteness, or unwillingness to seem like he was idle or some weird old-fella thing that mad bastards like Mickey and his grandfather would have in their heads. And finally Mickey answered and Lampy asked him would he get the old bus and bring it down to where he was, and he explained to Mickey what had happened, and Mickey said, I've a pint drank but I'll be okay, you're an awful man, how's it you couldn't drive it without breaking it? And Lampy breathed deep and clenched his fist and held himself level and forced himself to play along and he said, Ah, sure, you know me, and Mickey said he'd run up and get the old bus and he'd be down straight away and all they'd have to do would be transfer everybody over and if the Grogans didn't spot him he'd tell them nothing unless he had to, because they had an awful habit of apportioning blame to people even when there was no blame owed to anyone and they'd hardly be there anyway at this time on a Friday and it was a shame now he was going to miss the models on the *Afternoon Show* but how's ever, you can't have it every way and hold tight now and I'll be down pronto.

And Mickey was as good as his word. Lampy barely had the big Merc with the tinted windows backed neatly into a bay beside Con Kelleher's workshop and the keys left on the top of the back nearside tyre as per Mickey's advice, and with Mickey's promise to appraise Con of the situation, and everyone transferred over fine, and there wasn't a whole lot of giving out, and sticks and handbags were easily found, and Mr Collins declared that he was much happier in the old van, it was a much better proposition by far, and he stood beside Mickey as he looked into the engine bay of the Mercedes and they shook their heads in mournful unison and Mickey said, God only knows, could be anything, they'll have to get NASA to have a look at it, I'd say, or more likely they'll let Con hit it with a hammer until it goes again out of pure fright, and Mr Collins laughed and shook his stick at the offending engine with its new-fangled notions and its lack of simple integrity, and Mickey gave Mr Collins a hand onto the side ramp of the Transit and he said he'd give Con a shout now this minute and there was no need to worry about one thing except making the rest of the drops and the Transit was the best of them all and it was half full of diesel and if he had his way they'd still use the Transit as the main wagon and off you go now, good lad, and don't forget who gave you a dig-out, and tell your grandad I was asking for him and he still owes me a score. And Lampy drove on, faster now, relieved to be moving again, to be closer to having an empty bus for a while when he had Mr Collins and Mr Driscoll dropped to hydrotherapy and Mrs Bridges and Mrs Coyne dropped to physio and Mr and Mrs Chambers dropped to their daughter's house where they had dinner every Friday and Mrs Chambers always cried as she got back onto the bus, saying, Why can't we stay? Why can't we stay?

There was a quiet time each evening in the house. Once dinner was ate and Pop was settled, tutting, at the stove. The crackling flames and the ticking clock, Mam's rhythmic pounding of her dough, the darkening sky and the brightening moon, his heavy eyes. He would stretch along the couch and sometimes sleep. Lampy thought about the house now as he drove, about Pop and his mother and all the years that stretched into the distance ahead, formless and dull. Would he do this for ever? Drive buses and sit in day rooms and change sheets and talk to people while they wait to die? He felt like he'd stepped outside himself, somehow, replaced himself with this new incarnation, this strange, quiet man, this regretful person he didn't really know. He should have stayed in college, even though he'd picked a course he shouldn't have, civil engineering, because all the lads were doing it or something like it, and he'd given up on the idea of doing English or journalism, he'd never get the points no matter how many times he repeated, and he'd never told anyone about the things he really wanted to do.

Chloe wouldn't have left him if he'd had a degree, a posh job, a whack of money every week. Or every month: the posher your job the less often you get paid. But he couldn't manage the maths, and the assignments he submitted always came back with low grades and red biro marks all over them, and Cookie Ryan, whom he travelled in and out with, tried to give him a hand but the more he looked at things the less sense they made and he couldn't believe the amount of effort it took to just get one thing straight in his head, and then there'd be another thing waiting to be understood, and the queue of things waiting to be learned seemed to stretch to infinity, and one day he told Cookie not to bother calling for him next day and he'd see him at training on Thursday. And now Cookie and a few more of the lads were close enough to having their degrees and being actual engineers, and some of the jokes they made when they were out he didn't get, and he saw less and less of them as the months went by, and now he wasn't hurling either and there was a kind of an embarrassment between him and Cian Delahunty because they'd never really patched it up and so it was left there, the bad feeling and awkwardness, and he couldn't face it any more.

After Chloe broke it off, he applied for a job in a mine in Canada. It had seemed kind of heroic at the time, romantic almost; the hugeness of the idea of it blocked out the dull nausea Chloe's loss had left him with, the weakening gnaw in the centre of him. Pop, though, had made it sound foolish, embarrassing. Going off down a mine in – where's it again, the quare place? – northern Ontario? Jaysus. I could tip out as far as the quarry in Latteragh to see have they anything, wouldn't that do you if you're so intent on breaking rock? And Pop would poke a sod flame-ward and huff, and take off his reading glasses and put them back on, and make shapes to leave, and sit back down. And what could he do but look across at his red-faced grandfather, and up at the sorrowful eyes of Jesus and His bleeding Sacred Heart, and try to keep his patience while Pop raved on.

Where did you even get this fuckin idea? It's my own idea.

I hadn't to be given it. But one of the lads is going, Dean
Kelly. Kelly? My arse. Quarehawks, that crowd. None of them
ever even hurled. Plenty jobs here again now. Bobby Mahon
is mad looking for lads to work for him. What's taking you
to the North Pole is beyond me. It's nowhere near the North
Pole. I want to see some of the world. World? Isn't half the
fuckin world after landing here? You've only to go down
the town to see the whole world, these days. More in your
line stay here and marry a girl and have proper Irish children
before the foreign johnnies breed us out. Anyway, what'll
you see where you're going only snow and Eskimos? There'll
be no Eskimos. There will, of course. You'll be inside in
an igloo with them. All them lads live in igloos. They have
houses for the workers. They have. Houses made of snow.
Igloos. And he breathed deep in and slowly out until his temper settled and they sat in silence while Mam moved around
the rooms humming and Pop filled the empty space with
jokes.

Hey, while we're on the topic at all, what do you call a
house made out of snow that has no toilet? An ig! And talking
of snow, did I ever tell you about the poor old woman I came
across lying down in the snow there last year? Well, I presume
she was poor – she had only fifty-four cents in her purse! And
he'd laugh hard, because Pop was priceless at times, and when
he was on a roll of jokes the jokes were all that mattered, and
Chloe and Ontario and everything else faded back to nothing
for a while. Pop could make things up on the spot, yarns
and slags and bits of rhymes that would have you hardly able
to breathe from laughing. Like the day a few weeks ago he
was washing the Civic in the front yard and Pop was tipping
around out the back, straightening his bags of timber against

the side of the shed and tying back the branches of the rose-bushes to their trellises the way they'd be secured against the wind, and Pop had come around the front for some reason, and he'd noticed Pop had his waterproofs on backwards, and Pop had looked down at himself and then back up at Lampy and he's started singing:

> Me bollix is where me arse should be,
> They made me back to front, you see,
> Me bollix is where me arse should be,
> They made me back to front!

And Lampy had had to stop what he was doing and put down his soft-bristled brush and try to hold himself upright, and Mrs Delaney from two doors down was standing looking over, scowling, and Pop waved at her, a real cheeky waggle-fingered wave, and he'd said, Helloooo, in a squeaky, mocking voice before continuing the song that he was composing right there where he stood in the wet yard:

> I went to the doctor for to see
> Could anything be done for me.
>
> The doctor took one look at me,
> Says he, You're back to front!
> I know, says I, sure tis plain to see
> Me bollix is where me arse should be,
> The doctor says, Well, I will be,
> A crookedy-bollicky-cunt!
>
> That's what I am, says I to he,

And isn't it a tragedy,
That there could be a man like meeeeeee,
Whooooooose, bollix is back to front?

And Pop had really gone for it on the last two lines, running the notes up and up and on, like a mad whiskery opera singer, standing there in his backwards waterproof trousers and his wellingtons and his gardening gloves and his luminous walking coat, and Lampy had nearly puked from laughing.

He'd cancelled the whole Ontario thing the day he heard Pop talking to his mother about it from the hallway. Why does he think I killed myself buying out this house? Why I done three years extra abroad in the factory and my back broke? Lord, the money I gave the council just to say this place was ours, not to be always worried we'd be moved. And then having to pay myself for a front wall and a new roof when every other idler on the road got theirs for free. Why does he think I done that? The way there'd be something for him. Something he could say was his. A good start-off in life. There's no one will hand him a house out foreign. They'll use him to his bones then fuck him back and half his life gave down a hole. And something thrummed inside his head at Pop's tinny voice, and his stomach churned and burned with anger and guilt.

How could he tell his grandfather that he wanted to find a place where the measure of a man was different? Not linked to money or to sport or a road in a town. Or was it the same everywhere? He wanted to have no past, no address, to just be from Ireland. Not this town, or the Villas, or the house at the end of the terrace with the broken gatepost. He wanted to tell a romantic story to explain his father, to say that he was missing somewhere, in action maybe, last seen crossing an Afghan pass or a desert or a flooding river. Only Dean would know him in the mine and he'd go along with any story. Dean wouldn't judge him or think it was strange that he wanted to rewrite himself. Jesus, man, you're some liar, he'd say, and he'd be impressed. Anyway, he'd chickened out and so it was all the one now. Dean went on his own. He was sound enough about Lampy not going. Ah, fuck, Lamp, he said. I should have known you'd bail on me. Fuck, man. And Lampy just said he was sorry, he couldn't leave Pop and his mother alone, and Dean had said, All right, don't worry, I'll be grand, but he wondered afterwards exactly what Dean had meant when he said he should have known he'd bail. He saw a picture of him on Facebook in navy overalls and a heavy-looking helmet, standing smiling in a group of men before a mesh door. Going underground, it said beneath the picture, and Lampy wished when he saw the picture that he'd had the balls to go. To lower himself into the mantle of the earth.

He parked beside the door of the hydrotherapy centre and he got out and walked around and slid back the minibus door and he looked at Mr Collins, who was smiling at him, and he looked at Mr Driscoll, who was sitting behind Mr Collins, and Mr Driscoll was shaking his head at him and saying, They won't take us now, you should have rang them the minute we broke down, it's all gone to pot now, and Mrs Coyne was saying, Yerra will you whisht up out of it in the name of God, all you're going doing is dipping your arse in a pool of water, they've plenty water, it won't be dried up. And Mr Collins and Mr and Mrs Chambers laughed wheezily and Lampy laughed too and Mr Driscoll said nothing back to Mrs Coyne but he looked more shamefaced now than cross and he got up slowly from his seat, leaning heavily on his stick, and he followed Mr Collins to the side ramp and he held the bar tight while Lampy lowered it and Lampy put his hand on Mr Driscoll's arm as he stepped off the ramp, and Mr Driscoll looked straight into his eyes and Lampy could see something there, something he couldn't put a name on, some sort of an appeal for something but he couldn't say what, and then the thing was gone and his eyes narrowed and Mr Driscoll said, Thanks, Bighead, and he followed his bent comrade through the door of the hydrotherapy centre, stopping for a moment to coldly appraise the brawny attendant who was holding the door open for them.

Mrs Coyne's physio appointment was in a different part of the same building and they probably could have walked there because she was sprightly enough in spite of her arthritis or her healing hip or whatever it was she needed physio for, but he couldn't risk leaving Mr and Mrs Chambers in the bus on their own, and so he drove around and brought her to the reception area and she held his hand for support and he was embarrassed, then realized how ridiculous it was to feel embarrassed, and she called him lovey and told him not to mind that horrible old man, he hadn't an overly big head at all, nor had he big ears, he was a lovely-looking boy so he was and that old man was only jealous. And as he left her, she caught his hand again, and she drew him down so that he was stooped over her where she was sitting, and she craned her neck so that she could whisper into his ear, and she said, Because he's near to his death, you see, and he's afraid, and you're far from yours, and he wishes he had his life to live again, the way you have all of yours ahead of you to live.

Mr and Mrs Chambers' daughter's house was fifteen minutes away and they were already fifteen minutes late so Lampy knew he'd have to ring the home to ask them to ring the daughter to tell her he'd be late, because if it happened the other way round there'd be a faff and he'd have to explain about the broken-down bus and he wanted just to get the drop-offs and collections done and to get back to the home and do his day-room duty and then drive back around six to collect the Chamberses and he'd tell the Grogans about the bus in his own time because he couldn't listen to James Grogan's fake posh accent now, asking, What exactly happened, Laurence? and he'd draw out the *a* in exactly and the noise of it would be like brake callipers with worn pads closing on a disc, the kind of a noise that would madden you. Fuck the Grogans and their new shitbox bus. They probably bought it from a write-off merchant, it was probably written off up the North or in England or somewhere and cleared through Customs for half nothing and stuck back together and re-plated. Just like they cut corners on nurses and care assistants and food and cleaning equipment and God knows what else and stretched everyone to their limits and asked him to supervise the day room and drive the bus and he not really qualified to do either thing, and probably not even insured if it came to it, but James Grogan was from a long line of crooks, white-toothed, shiny-shoed priests and politicians and shopkeepers and auctioneers and accountants and landowners and builders; and Lampy had no such pedigree, no such august lineage.

Bridie answered. No problem. She'd let them know he was on his way. Lampy breathed in and out and relaxed into the drive. There was a sparkle here and there from the tarmac and the reading on the dash was minus one, and Mrs Chambers hummed behind him, a tuneful hum, a familiar song though he couldn't name it, and he could see in the rear-view mirror that her eyes were closed and her husband was looking out the window and smiling to himself, and her head was inclined towards him so that her forehead was almost resting on his shoulder, and they were gone daft, the both of them, he knew, but he liked looking at them all the same. How must it feel, he wondered, to be at the brink of death, and still to have to live each ordinary day through? Does a panic rise unbidden now and then, a terror of the moment of passing? It's the moment before he'd be most afraid of, the moment of complete and terminal awareness, the constriction of his lungs, the burning want for air, or the shuddering of his heart or the popping of the valves inside his brain or the breaking of his neck or the impact with the bridge abutment or the rush of the air past his face as he fell or the coldness of the black rushing water flowing back from the city and up towards its own source, its own point of beginning.

The Chamberses' daughter stood beside the idling bus in the front yard of her house. Monstrous evergreens lined the driveway and fortressed the garden from the road, and the house was massive, red-bricked, many-windowed. A child of eight or nine stood in the open door, three steps up from the gravel. Lampy got out to assist with the couple's disembarking, and the daughter thanked him; she looked pretty and weary and she was wearing a tight hoodie over skinny jeans and she seemed younger than he remembered and she was in wicked shape and he hadn't remembered noticing this about her on previous drops or collections. Maybe she'd been wearing looser clothes. She had her arms folded tight below her breasts against the cold and she looked at his T-shirt and she said, You're very hot in yourself, and he took a moment to realize that she meant he was wearing clothes you'd wear on a hot day, and she looked at him a second or two longer than seemed normal and he wondered was she one of these middle-aged women who have rich husbands who can't get it up because they're too stressed or too fat, and he felt himself hardening again and he nearly pulled Mr Chambers down off the ramp before slamming the sliding door closed.

And Lampy Shanley had an empty bus, and all he had to do now was drive slowly back to the orthopaedic hospital and wait for Mrs Coyne at the physio outpatients centre and then swing round to the hydrotherapy unit for Mr Happy and Mr Crappy and collect the Chamberses and then he could pop them back to the home and park up the wagon and leave a note for the Grogans about the Merc being in Con Kelleher's yard and they might actually praise him for his smooth handling of the whole thing, his decision not to bother them with it, just to ring Mickey Briars and sort it sensibly and efficiently, and then he could go home and check the oil and the coolant and the brake fluid in the Civic and give it a bit of a clean-out on the inside and check how many condoms he had in the glovebox and have a shit and a shave and a shower and a good careful wash of his bits because he didn't know yet what kind of shapes Eleanor might make, what moves she had waiting for him, and he felt a fizzing thrill of pleasure, and he looked up at himself in the rear-view mirror and he looked back at himself from the mirror and he looked all right, like a lad doing a good day's work who had a good night's work ahead of him, and then he heard, as though she were there in the minibus with him, sitting beside him, pushing her blonde hair back from her face, blinking her blue-green eyes at him, Chloe, saying, I'm sorry, Lampy, It's not you, it's me, I just don't love you, I don't love you.

And he looked down at his hands on the steering wheel, and at the dash where the temperature reading was minus three, and then at the cold, empty road where ice was forming in the rivulets between the tarmac's stones, smoothening the surface, divesting it of grip, so that it could coolly reject the advances of the old bus's threadbare tyres, and he saw the corner of the gable wall of the old mill at the bend of the road ahead, the arrowed V of the corner of the gable, thick block, ancient and unyielding, and he couldn't hear the engine any more, or the swish of the tyres on the road, or the wind blowing through the dried-out door seals; all he could hear was his heartbeat, and it was strong and regular and loud in his ears, a boom-booming sound, and briars poked like long fingers from the hedges on both sides, crooked in accusation, or in mockery, or both, and the hedges were whitening fast and the grass was flecked and frigid on the verges, and all things in the world were still but him, and he was hurtling through that still world and his right foot was pushing downwards and he could hear Jim Gildea at the door of his house, telling Pop and Mam there'd been an accident, it was Laurence, he skidded on ice, the bad bend by the mill, it was a terrible accident, a terrible, terrible accident.

And the corner of the gable of the mill wall was still a hundred yards away. And he saw his mother standing by the window looking out, looking for him. He saw her ageing, shrinking, curling into herself, lines forming on her face. He saw her at sixty-five, twenty years a grieving mother. Her hair gone white and wispy, pulled into a bun. Her looks gone. He knew she was a looker: the lads all slagged him over it. Some of their mothers were awful heaps of yokes. She was careful about herself, she went to a spin class and she walked and swam. She went on dates now and then with red-faced apologetic men. There was a foreigner from the hospital she went for drives with. He thought of how little he knew about her, for all the time they'd spent beside each other, for all the nights he'd slept curled into her. He thought of her saying, He's twenty years gone. He saw her sitting at the table with Pop, silent, and then without Pop, saying, Daddy never got over it, you know. It killed him. And his heartbeat eased and the noise of the tyres on the road came back and the clattering engine and the wind through the perished seals. And he eased his foot back up from the throttle and he braked gently into the bend and he drove smoothly out of it, and the mill wall's image diminished in his mirror and his mind, and he wondered would he waste much diesel if he left the engine running while he waited at the centre for the passengers, because if he killed it he'd have no heater and he'd only brought his hoodie and no hat, and he wondered why he was worried about the Grogans' diesel, fuck them, but it was probably from force of habit because he was always worried about the petrol gauge in the Civic, and whether he was going to make it home. He often used the petrol from Pop's jerry-can in the shed when he was stuck and he'd hear Pop cursing out the back when he went to fill the mower or his strimmer or his chainsaw and he'd shout in the back door, Hye, cuntyballs, did you use the last of my juice? and Lampy would always laugh at the word cuntyballs, Pop's worst insult, the one he used for only the most terrible of offences, and he'd walk to the Topaz and refill the can and Pop would yank it from his hands when he got back and call him a bollix but he'd be over it by then, he'd have roses deadheaded or corner weeds pulled during the wait for the petrol, or a sparrowhawk spotted across the fields, high and still, wings spread, waiting to thrust itself downward, to pluck some tiny creature from the earth.

John

THERE'S GOD. There's God now, do you see Him? I know it's only Venus, but I may as well call her God, a perfect ball of blooming fire in the sky above us, winking over at the early risen moon. If God is everything it may as well be Him there when I look up, His presence centred on that shining whiteness. The Muslim boys say all is divine, every miserable and mundane and magnificent thing, and who am I to argue, after all I've done? The frost makes Him brighter. I could say I'm only a tool of omnipotence, a wretched object beset by Fate. I could say no importance should be ascribed to me or to my thoughts or deeds: I'm only an actor who learned by rote and said what lines were given to him. Lord God, I wish that was true, then there'd be no confessions needed, and we could rest here and keep each other company in peace.

I used to be so steady and so strong. No rigour now have I except in thought. This quivering place I occupy, this weak republic, soon will fall. I have to say some things before I go. I feel the breath of angels on my neck. Their breath is foul. They're from the other legion, I'd say. O Father. Father. Will you hear my confession? If I whisper it to you, will you just hear it? I don't know the ritual any more, the words that once were scored across my mind, standing out in bright relief each time I closed my eyes. I was always so afraid of saying them wrong, you see. A solecism in my speech would become an erratum on some celestial scroll, I thought, and I'd be flayed for ever for it in the fires of Hell. O Lord God, the things I believed. At one of my earliest confessions, it could have been my first, I suppose, I couldn't remember my Act of Contrition. Come on, said the priest, I haven't all day. Say the Act of Contrition. And I was silent, studying the floor before my knees and the toes of his shiny black shoes. He was sitting on the end of a pew and I was kneeling in the side aisle of Ardnamoher Church, the throw of a stone from my primary school and a field from my father's house. We hadn't confessionals that time. I paid to have them installed years later, heavy mahogany contraptions with an opaque mesh between compartments, with padding for the penitent's knees and a soft seat for the confessor's arse. But this priest wasn't to know I'd one day be a knight, and he was old and cantankerous, though not a bad man. I thought you were all taught this in school? We were, Father, I whispered. What's that? We were, Father. Well, why can't you say it, then? I don't know, Father, I just can't remember it. Can't you, faith. Maybe you didn't listen while it was being taught. Maybe I'll have to have a word with Miss Fahy about you. Now, I'll give you one last chance.

But not one word of the Act of Contrition could I remember. And I having sung it sweetly only hours before in school, before we were shepherded to our ordeals. His great red face and grizzled jaw, his pitch-black cassock and his burnished shoes, the smell of ferment off him like maggoty windfalls, all conspired to strike me blank and dumb. And he wasn't of a mind to give a prompt, though I knew if I heard the opening phrase I'd be away, and I'd deliver it straight and clear, without quaver or tremor or pause. Well, if you can't give me an Act of Contrition, I can't give you absolution, he said, and so you'll have to leave this place still heavy with sin. Go on now, gather yourself up and go back to your classmates and see how your burden weighs you down. And I thought of the Commandments I'd broken, and I couldn't face the suffering Christ as I knelt alongside the other penitents who had known their Act by heart and spoken true, and so I hung my head low so as to avoid the agonied face of the Son of God, the sight of His racked body pierced by nails, and I moved my lips as though reciting my prayers of atonement, and I thought how I was adding sin to sins, by kneeling there pretending to have been forgiven, and I waited for the old priest's hairy hand to close around the back of my shirt collar and drag me away, out through the door of the church and into the cold yard.

Enough of that, of childish terror and ancient foolishness. I'll whisper out my sins to you and you can hear them, anyway, and this confessional is fine and wide, not like the upright coffins sometimes used, and the quietness around us here is deep, and the quietness seems to have a purpose about it, the expectant stillness of a held breath, a pause for a search for a felicitous word, a consoling gesture, a heartening smile or nod. Bless me, Father, for I have sinned. I'll tell you them in order, one by one, and the roll of them is short, though each one might be made of a hundred parts or more.

This is not my father's confession but mine, and I'm offering this not in mitigation but only by way of explanation. My father lost his first and best-loved son and shortly after started buying land. As though to allow accommodation for the breadth and expanse of his sorrow. He'd have bought the world if it was offered him, and left it fallow and empty. He pushed the boundaries of our farm up the walls of the valley and down the far side, across the main road and the bog in Annaholty to the foot of Keeper Hill. He bought fields of deep rich soil and green grass meant for grazing, he bought acres of rocky scrub and briars, he bought marshy worthless tracts in the floodplain of the Dead River between Keeper Hill and the Mother Mountain. He attended every auction and men would see him coming and throw their eyes to Heaven and their hats at the enterprise; they knew he wouldn't be outbid. The disinterested nephews of dead bachelors were guaranteed a quick sale and a good price. I watched him one day at the bar of a pub near Newport, drinking whiskey after whiskey with a man whose speech was slurring and whose eyes were glazed and red. I saw him lay a pile of banknotes down, and tap them with his finger twice, and push them under the drunk man's nose. I watched the drunk man offer his hand and tell my father he was a decent skin and toast his health. And my father smiled and he patted the man's back as he turned away from the bar and his empty glass, back to his half-life of silent, gentle frenzy.

I was given a tour of the vaults of a bank one time years later by a man who said he didn't believe in God. A squat man, but handsome in his way, with silver hair and steady eyes and a charming smile. He put gold in my hand, that shining standard, a bar of it, and I felt its coldness on my skin, leaking into me. Science would say the opposite should happen, that the heat of my body should have warmed that metal where I touched it, but gold has its own rules, it seems. I asked him what the bar was worth, and he said, Forty thousand pounds, and I bought it from him there and then. I paid that little alchemist by cheque and his smile was the same as it always was as he folded my cheque away and handed me my gold inside a small roped bag. I kept the bar of gold inside a combination-locked briefcase inside a safe that was set in the floor of my office, snug in the concrete. I took it out every now and then, and I set it on my desk and I twined my fingers together and looked at it. It shone no matter what the light. I lowered my face down onto it sometimes, and rested my cheeks against it, and thought how anyone watching would think me a madman, bowed and prone in a business suit, but my office had no windows and its door was always locked. I marvelled always at its coldness, how its frigid aspect belied its malleability, its ductile nature.

Often I took that gold and laid it across the palms of my hands and lifted it, and closed my eyes, and I'd imagine the intercession I wished for, the small variation I wanted made, and when I opened my eyes again a calf was always standing on my hands, placid and sinewed, graven by some magic from the gold, gleaming in that lightless place. And as often as not my prayed-for thing would come to pass. Now what do you think of that? All the gold in the mantle and the crust of the earth fell from the heavens. That's a fact. It came in a bombardment, four billion years ago, flung down from the darkness, from the spaces between stars.

My brother's name was Edward. O Father, if you'd seen him. He was beautiful, even I knew that, and I only a wobbling grey gosling in the corner of the field he commanded, adoring him. I knew my parents loved him best and I didn't care; sure, how could it have been otherwise? I always saw the things people thought they'd concealed fully; I had a devilish knack for it. Edward was six years older than me and he was kind to me always, as he was to little Henry and to Julie and to Connie, who was three years younger than him and who worshipped him like I did, only with a more fervent intensity, a strange unsettling love. She'd follow him from room to room and moon over him, sitting quietly pretending to be reading while he studied or listened to the radio but I knew she was watching him, his lips moving as he read, a habit he had, like he wasn't a strong reader even though he was – he read books my father wouldn't have been able for, about science and history and all the things that happened and the ways people lived in faraway parts of the world – or laughing or whistling in amazement at something that was funny on the radio or shocking in the news, and she'd say, What? What is it? And he'd explain to her, patiently, the thing he'd been laughing at or amazed by, and she'd say, Oh, that's really funny, Ed, or Oh, that's really interesting, Ed, and Julie and Henry and I would smirk behind our hands and she'd pinch us if she caught us and tell us to get out, we were disturbing Edward and it wasn't fair.

I don't think my brother Edward was able to commit a sin. He hurled and kicked football in a way that brought tears to old men's eyes. He picked up Irish like another boy would pick up the baiting of a hook or the raising of a sliotar; he was a true Gael in learning and manner and strength. The teachers at school were nearly jealous of him. We drove one day to Thurles for the minor county final; we were in the lead car, Daddy and Edward, the captain, and me and a burlap sack of hurls, and I stared at him that whole winding way down to Semple Stadium. He only smiled at me now and again and squeezed my leg or punched my arm gently in play. He was quiet; I thought he must be nervous. Expectation must have weighed on him, although you'd never have thought it if you hadn't known him like I did, every mannerism and tic and way of talking and of being silent. He hurled that day like a supernatural thing; he scored before him and was lifted off the field and applauded and cheered, even by the opposition, and going home in the car he turned a kind of a pale, sickly colour and he told my father he didn't feel great and Daddy asked did he want him to stop and Edward said, no, he'd be grand, and Daddy said, Let me know, son. You played your guts out. I wouldn't blame you for feeling sick.

When we arrived into the yard at home Edward's leg betrayed him getting out of the car and he fell onto the flags and he died there where he fell. There's a spark that burns inside the heart that fuels its beating. Doctors know little about the working of it and less again about its random sudden extinguishing, only that it sometimes stutters and winks out without warning in the hearts of the fit and young. That's what happened to Edward: all that long road home from the county final that tiny flame was being quenched and relit, as though darkness and light waged war on one another in his chest. And in the end, as dear Edward stepped from Daddy's car and my mother watched out the kitchen window with a smile of welcome already on her lips, darkness won. My father stood outside in the yard that night and roared curses at the heavens and my mother sat whitely on a chair alongside Edward's bed with her rosary beads, and I crept upstairs and knelt on the floor outside that sacred room and repeated my father's curses word for word, and meant them, down to the centre of me. I cursed and blasphemed and swore and railed against Him, and never once repented for that yet. The Lord won't hold me guiltless, Father, will He? That endlessly bargaining God, that meticulous exacter of tolls.

The Lord won't hold me guiltless for I took His name in vain. And never in the offhand way of the thoughtlessly profane, cursing at the flight of a ball or the turn of a card or some sudden mishap: I revelled in it; I knew what I was saying, what I was doing. Things that some men say by rote and habit I said with malignant design, with relish: God, blast you. God, damn. Damn you, God, damn you. You know how this would go if I went on. I hated that jealous God who visited the iniquities of the fathers on the children to the third and fourth generations, even while He showed mercy to thousands, to all those who loved Him and kept His Commandments. I watched Him visit iniquity; He did it in my father's yard, before my eyes.

It was a Sunday that my brother died and never after was it kept holy. My father continued to go to Mass and observe holy days of obligation, and folded notes into collections for the priests of the parish and the upkeep of the church, and my mother was unstinting in her duties and was always at his side, or a half a step behind him, but inside the boundaries of our farm there was no God; He was cast out, evicted, and all His pious furnishings destroyed. Statues carved or cast of stone or clay were smashed to pieces on the flags of the yard. Pictures of the Sacred Heart were ripped from their frames and the frames were snapped and kindled and the pictures and the frames were stacked and burned. The same flames will lick the flesh from your bones some day, my mother told my father, as he stoked the bonfire, and your flesh will grow back to be flayed away again, over and over for all of eternity. I don't care, my father told her, I don't care. And my mother said no more to him, just walked back into her kitchen and her chores, pale and bent from sorrow.

So I took my lead where it was given and I never remembered the Sabbath day, nor did I keep it holy. Six days I laboured always, all my life, and did all my work, and the seventh day I kept for myself solely, for my especial interests. In truth I did the best part of my life's work on the seventh day of every week, and my wife, and my daughters, and every man and woman that ever worked for me, and every stranger that was ever within my gates was harried into motion on that day, roused early and set to their tasks. The Lord busied Himself making the heavens and the earth and the sea and all that is in them and rested on the seventh day, and therefore He blessed the Sabbath day and hallowed it, and I kept my worst excesses for that day.

My days weren't long upon the land my father bought. I never honoured him, nor did I honour my mother. And still I tried in every way to be a perfect son. I worked hard at my lessons and I read the books left thumbed and dog-eared by

Edward, though I could hardly make head or tail of some of them, and I practised my Irish and my Latin and I hurled an hour at least each day in the long acre, pucking the sliotar high and catching it, running myself into the ground, collapsing exhausted at the end of the hour onto the rich, yielding earth. I remembered Edward playing hurling and my father roaring and screaming and breaching the sideline and threatening referees and breaking hurleys off of the ground in frustration or anger or joy. When I played, he watched in silence. Win or lose, he was quietly accepting. The odd day, he'd put his hand on my back as we walked to the car after I came out of the dressing room and my heart would soar. Then I'd wonder was he only doing that opposite the neighbours, and my doubt in him would stiffen my spine and he'd take his hand away.

The more heed I took of his passionless presence, well back from the field's edge, hands in his coat pockets or arms tightly crossed, the more I concentrated on what I was doing. And so my game never flowed, my deliberateness only translated into mistake after stupid mistake. I fumbled and tripped and swung wildly and cowered reflexively when I should have stood my ground, like Edward would have. And soon enough I was on the subs' bench and never started, then got no game at all, and for a finish wasn't even selected for the panel for what would have been my second year playing at under-sixteen. And I was relieved. I'd never again have to sit beside him in the car on the journey home with the ghost of my brother Edward sitting in the silence between us.

I had none of Edward's courage, though I tried and tried to make myself be brave. My father brought me once to town to help him nail election placards to lampposts. He was doing his damnedest to get a man called John Joe Burke elected into a seat left vacant by the unexpected death of an old soldier of destiny who'd held the seat for a lifetime. The old soldier had no son to be shooed into the seat, and his daughter was of no repute and not talked about. My father wanted to fill the seat with a proxy; he'd been worrying lately about the threat of compulsory purchase orders, the wounds they could inflict upon his sprawling fields, and John Joe Burke could be relied upon to scupper any plans for roads or railways or estates of houses on my father's vast repining plain.

I was thirteen, long-legged and gangly and prone to a violent reddening and an intractable mumbling when addressed by anyone bar my mother. I was strong, though, broad of shoulder and big of hand, and was well able for the labour, though slow and fumbling: I'd had a sudden shot of growth that summer and wasn't wearing it well. I was up a ladder at the market square end of Silver Street. There were two men standing at the rails outside the bank on the far corner of the square, one facing me across the road with one foot on the lower rail and his elbows resting on the upper. His comrade leaned with his back to the rails and viewed my toiling image in the bank's high glass door. The four streets that converged at that spot were empty save for me and them; it was early on a September Saturday, the sun was barely up. I was on my ladder's second-highest step, proud of my daring, hammering happily. I thought they would just rest there in smirking observation of the work in the manner, I knew even then, of all corner-boys, until the one with his foot on the rail began to speak, loud enough so that I could clearly hear him. Do you remember that story, he asked his friend, about the three little republicans that were putting up posters above in Drumcondra at the very end of the civil war? I do, the friend replied, after giving the query a few seconds' consideration, I remember Brother Frank telling us all about it, God rest him. Weren't they about that boy's age over there, above on that ladder? They were, I'd say. Was it Charlie Dalton of the Squad that shot them or who was it? It was Charlie Dalton, right enough, one of Michael Collins's boys. He riddled them with bullets from a confiscated gun, the poor little puddlahauns!

And they both snorted with laughter and the first speaker hawked and spat on the road, and when I looked down and across at them I saw in the bank's door the reflection of the one with his back to me, as he slowly pulled something long and darkly metallic from inside his jacket. My breath caught in my throat and I saw that my knuckles were white from the fierceness of my grip on my hammer and the ladder's top edge. I felt a blooming of warmth in my crotch as fear loosened my bladder. These men were going to shoot me, like the little lads above in Dublin all those years ago, and my father was streets and streets away and my mother was at home baking tarts, a platoon of sausages and rashers already assembled on the warming grill pan for the breakfast I would never eat.

And then my father strode across the road from the doorway of O'Halloran's the undertakers where he must have been standing unseen all along. My young heart sang at the sight of him and in the same second lurched in fear that he would be killed in my stead and in the next second broke at the realization that I was a coward. My father's face was a furious, pulsing red; his fists were clenched. The man whose foot was on the railing straightened up all of a shot and his eyes were wide with the shock of my father's sudden appearance. Ye dirty fucking blackguards. I heard ye, ye dirty fucking blackguards, trying to frighten the boy. The one that was facing away had

The cold slows the blood. Stillness makes things worse. A man would want to be moving around to keep it flowing, striding and stamping, stoking the heat in his muscles. There's not much space for that in this box. My legs haven't the will anyway. If you are the voice and hand of God on earth you're doing a fair passable impression of the man Himself; you're as silent as He and as dark. I wonder can you hear me at all, or if it even matters. Isn't my contrition all the point, my throwing down of myself, my prostration before the chance of mercy? I never could talk about two things: regret or love. You're a cold conduit, Father, and maybe that's best. I wonder if I'm even talking at all. Which or whether I'll persevere; the telling of these tales is taking something from me, something I'm as well off relinquishing, something I held to myself too long.

As I've told you about my brother Edward I may as well tell you about my sister Connie. She turned wicked in her grief for him. What are you crying about? she hissed into my ear at Edward's graveside, as he disappeared from my eyes into the waiting ground. You hardly knew him. And when I looked up at her she had darkness in her eyes as black as her funeral clothes, and her rage and her grief had coloured her face white. The contrast was vivid, like my shock; her words fair whipped. She was a womanly fourteen, and I noticed then for the first time how beautiful she was, dark-haired and elegant, dangerously proportioned. I stopped my tears and felt ashamed of them. I brushed them off my face and shed no more for my dear brother that day. She had regard for none of us, my mother or my father or my other sister Julie, who was a year younger than me, or my little brother Henry, who came along behind us all as an afterthought, a tiny, soundless incarnation of a short renaissance in my parents' feelings for one another. He was always scared, his smallness and his way of slinking about unseen, inhabiting the background like a soft hiss of white noise behind the ceaseless hum and hubbub of life, even the curtailed, nervy life we lived after Edward, like an apology for his accidental existence. Connie tormented us all, but Henry the most. She tortured him. And I let her, gladly.

Edward's death extinguished whatever bit of a flame was rekindled between my parents that led to poor Henry's appearance on this earth. I don't think they ever saw each other again after they walked hand in hand from the Height the day Edward was lowered into the wounded ground, only existed silently beside each other for half a lifetime, looking inwards. There was the odd explosion, like the day of the poster-nailing inside in Nenagh – or have I told you that story? – or the time my mother had a fight with a young curate who came to the house uninvited one Sunday evening shortly after Edward died to offer the solace of his ministries. He glanced and glanced again at the unstained square of wall where the Sacred Heart picture had hung and in the end could contain himself no longer and asked why had it been taken down, and Mother said she couldn't stand to be smirked at by a Jew. And the curate stood and shouted, God forgive you, woman, the tongue on you, you should be ashamed, there's no grief great enough to allow for that kind of talk out of a Christian, and my mother said calmly that she needed no forgiveness, especially not from a snotty-nosed child like him, and he wasn't to darken her door again.

So Connie was given a free rein to gallop about the house, organizing and bossing and screeching and cornering Henry whenever he came into her view to tell him he was nothing only a burden on the whole family and an embarrassment and a gimpy pup who should have been drowned at birth only Mammy and Daddy hadn't had the heart and so they'd fished him back out of the trough outside beside the haggard wall and let him live and didn't they regret their foolish kindness now that they had to look at him creeping about the place like a horrible crawly yoke? And Henry would say nothing back ever, only cringe, eyes closed, his shoulders hunched up so high and tight that it seemed as though he were trying to draw his whole head inside his body, like a tortoise. He'd stick an elbow straight out from himself as a static and ineffective defence, his lips drawn back from his little white teeth in a deathly grimace. I watched with glee while she dissected him. I had no brother only Edward in my child's mind; Henry was an impostor, an aberration, he didn't deserve a life. I willed nightly that Edward be resurrected and his place in the ground taken by Henry, or for time to be folded back on itself and for Henry's heart to be cursed with the aberrant flame and not Edward's. I promised votive offerings in my prayers, all sorts and sizes of them, if I could wake some morning to the sound of a sliotar being pucked against the end wall of the barn.

The odd day she was left fully in charge of us, Connie would assemble us, me and Julie and Henry, on the green couch with the sculpted wooden legs in the good room and she'd close the muslin curtains behind us so that the yellow-filtered, watery sunlight would spill onto our heads and she'd stand before us and pour scorn and fury on us. Look at ye. Fucking turnip-heads. Thank God I'm not related to ye. I'm adopted, you know. A friend of Daddy's who works for the government telephoned to know would he and Mammy come and bring Edward and me from our real parents' castle on a mountainside in Bavaria. I was only a new-born. Our real father was an archduke. Our mother was a Russian princess. They went against Hitler and were captured and sent away to a labour camp. We were hidden by the servants down in their village. Ye have nothing to do with us. Ugly little fatsos. Ugly little Irish pudding-faces.

And Julie's eyes would widen and she'd break into giggles and clap a little hand over her mouth to stifle herself and Connie would kick her full force into the shin or slap her pretty face or pinch her tender underarm and make her scream, a silent exhalation, the sudden, shocking pain stripping the sound from her roars. She'd jab Henry in his weak little concave chest with a savage, aristocratic finger and say, You killed my brother, you disgusting little creature, he was carrying you around on his shoulder the morning of his county final, you dirty little animal, he strained his heart carrying you around the yard that morning to please you and you oinking like a piglet and pissing in your breeches all over his back, you smelly little murdering bastard, you killed the handsome son of an archduke of Bavaria who faced down the Nazis and you'll pay dearly some day.

And then she'd stand and draw out her full height and there'd be a haze of muted light around her, rendering her even more unearthly, motes of dust dancing around her head like startled fairies, and she'd regard us silently: Henry sobbing,

Julie caressing her shin or forearm, her breath hitching, her narrow little back shuddering, and Connie's gaze would fall on me. And you, you changeling. You're evil. I saw you from the kitchen window that day Daddy drove into the yard. You stepped out of the car and walked over Edward as he lay dying and you barely glanced at him. You smelt your dinner cooking, all you wanted was to fill your greedy guts, you creep, you shit, you rat from Hell, you have no heart and no soul and some day soon you'll be going back to Hell where you belong and the devil will stick a big roasting fork up your greedy arse.

But I was well able for her. I enjoyed the good-room speeches. That pierced her. She could say what she wanted to me because I knew the truth of who I was and what I felt; Julie and Henry hadn't the same sense of themselves. I thrilled as she scourged their souls, I drank their blood. I'd tire of her and break the spell, though, eventually: Go way and fuck off, Connie, you're no German princess, you're a big fat Irish heifer. And me and Edward were forever calling you a mad cow behind your back and laughing about your big fat arse. And she'd fall on me in a frenzy, scratching and biting and slapping with all her might, growling and spitting and hissing and pulling clumps of my hair out by the roots, and Julie and Henry would spirit themselves away from the vicious melee to their rooms where they'd curl into balls and read their books and hug their teddy bears. And I'd just throw my forearm across my eyes so she wouldn't blind me and let her wear herself out. I don't know what name you'd put on that sin, my not minding little Henry, but it torments me still and there it is confessed anyway.

There was a boy whose mother had been a beauty queen in my class at school. I saw him one day walking with her on a street in Nenagh. She was laughing at something he was saying and the sound of her laugh was like thin glass breaking on stone and she had most of her looks kept and she wore no headscarf but her hair was blonde and wavy like a film star's and she touched his arm as she laughed and he looked pleased with himself and a man approached them and they all three stood talking and laughing and the man put his hand on both their arms and gestured with a nod towards the other end of the street, and he guided them back the way they had come and they walked towards the door of the Hibernian Inn and I watched from the shadow of the central pillar outside Gough, O'Keeffe and Naughton's department store as the boy from my class whose name was Sanders held the door for his mother and his father and the three of them stepped in to take their lunch.

His father and my father were friends, I don't know why. Shortly after that day I saw him with his parents in Nenagh he read out a poem in Brother Alphonsus Keane's English class he'd composed about the Norman invasion. I remember the words of the first verse to this day.

> *Armoured they came from the east,*
> *From a low and quiet sea.*

We were a naked rabble, throwing stones;
They laughed, and slaughtered us.

He read it sweetly; there was a kind of music in his voice. You could nearly imagine the naked Irish watching in dumb wonderment as the monstrous Norsemen, all metal vests and flashing broadswords, swept regally up along the beach towards them, while the ignorant rabble scrabbled around on the ground for something to fling at them.

There were long, silent seconds in the classroom after he'd finished. Brother Alphonsus broke the quietness. That's beautiful, Jonathan. Old Alphonsus was mad for it, of course. I pushed that Sanders boy into a corner of the yard after. There were four or five lugs behind me, sensing blood, giddy and giggling. I'd become a bit of a schoolyard bully in my early teenage years. Who's *we*? I asked him. He was tall, tending towards lanky, he hadn't the full of himself yet got, and his customary assuredness was after leaving him in short order. A sudden redness bloomed in his pale cheeks and moistness blurred his eyes. A fog formed on the lenses of his glasses. From my breath or the heat of his fear, I wasn't sure. Who's this *we* in your beautiful poem? I asked again. Who's this holy fucking *us*? He kept his head up and stayed looking at me from under his glasses, down along his long, thin nose. He was frightened but no coward. I wanted him to feel scorned; his haughty silence scalded me.

You're nothing to do with us, I said. And then I stepped back and drew a kick square into his balls as hard as I could. He doubled over and fell slowly forward, clutching himself, making a low, whiny noise. I hit him again as he fell, with my fist on the back of his head, but my heart had gone from it. My point was made; I walked away. I spat on the ground as I went, like I'd seen someone do in a film, a tough guy who was after winning a fight. The lugs all laughed. That Sanders boy who wrote the lovely poem, who was born and reared not three miles from my father's yard, lay moaning softly on the frost-hardened muck behind me. I kicked him in the balls that day because he said *we* but he meant *me*. I kicked him because of his goodness, too, and because he put me in mind of the things I wasn't, because of his beautiful smiling mother and his affable dapper father and his calm untroubled air. That Sanders boy got an awful time from that day on. I always had a fiendish knack for making people hate each other. I made out to all who'd listen, and nearly everyone listened to me, that his ancestors had been given land for favours done for and information given to Cromwell's officers; he was a son of a son of a son of colluders with the Roundheads, the filthy Cromwellites, who pitched babies into the air and caught them on the bayonets of their muskets, who nailed priests to rough crosses, who raped and ravaged and murdered all up and down this land. In those days, not so many days ago, and in that place, not so many miles from here, factiousness was rampant, hate came easy.

It was from the experience of blackening that boy that I learned an important and valuable lesson: if you say something enough times, the repetition of it makes it true. Any notion you like, no matter how mad it seems, can be a fact's chrysalis. Once you say it loud enough and often enough it becomes debatable. Debates change minds. Debate is the larval stage of truth. Constant, unflagging, loud repetition completes your notion's metamorphosis into fact. The fact takes wing and flutters from place to place and mind to mind and makes a living, permanent thing of itself. I said an ancestor of his was one of the notorious Limerick businessmen who sent a million sides of bacon and a million firkins of butter and ship after ship after ship near capsizing with corn off to England and to Europe and to God knows where else during the famine, during Ireland's great hunger, while country people and city people alike died in ditches, their mouths all green from eating grass. That's his stock, I said, that's them all out, and are you surprised he's writing love songs to Strongbow?

Some of the boys with more independent minds argued the long and the short of it. Two sides formed but one side gave ground quickly. He's a traitor for sure. He's not, he's grand, what did he ever do? He wrote a poem about how great the English are. That's not what it was about. His people were landlords; they only turned Catholic years ago to spite their own. They weren't, his father has only thirty acres. Their big house was burned by the rebels long ago and most of their land taken off them by the Land Commission. What big house? It's gone, sure, it was burned to the ground. They're all traitors all back along, that crowd. What about his poem? Calling us all naked savages and making out the Normans were the bee's knees? He's a queer too, I'd say. He's a traitor and a queer. He is, so he is. A traitor and a queer. And so that's what the boy became in the minds of his schoolmates, by virtue of constant repetition.

That was the seal broken on my bearing of false witness against my neighbours. And I made an art form of it. I met a man on a narrow street one day years later who was locking the door of his car and I startled him with my greeting, and he swung around and looked me in the eye, and I could see he had an inkling who I was, and I watched as his face washed itself of expression and he stood and looked and I started to try to read him, and to calculate his price, but he had closed himself completely to my view. Can I walk with you? I asked him, and he nodded his assent. We talked about the weather and the closeness of Christmas, and we marvelled at the galloping of time. It only feels like last week it was Christmas, and we laughed. And I asked him had he made his mind up on a planning application in which a client of mine had an interest, and he looked at me and looked up at the sky and he said, I think it's cold enough for snow. Do you? And I saw the truth of him behind his smile, the settled, attentive, uxorious husband, the loving, interested father, the loyal friend, the timely settler of debts, the steady, honest marker of time, the *t*-crosser, the *i*-dotter, the easy sleeper. And I saw reflected in his eyes a bedraggled man, a thing not a man at all. I saw myself as this honest man saw me, and I sensed the pity he had for me, the fear he had of me, and I hated him. I'd say it is, I said. We'll have snow on the ground in the morning for sure.

So I met him again at the launch of a book by a man we both knew who'd played hurling. And I asked him to hear a proposal I had about some work he could do on the side, some consultancy work, all above board and quotable to the taxman if he so wished, or the fee could be lodged to an account on an island in the Caribbean and easily and unnoticeably drawn on, and the fee would be two hundred thousand pounds. And this was 1989 and six-figure sums were only fairy stories, and we were standing side by side at the back of the function room and a man was orating the hero on the stage and the hero looked uncomfortable and shy, not like he'd looked when he'd lifted cups, roaring with the crowd, with blood on his face and the muck of the pitch. And the man I had been paid to persuade to make a certain decision regarding the zoning of land coughed a little and caught himself and whispered, How much? And again I said, Two hundred thousand pounds. And I felt a shift, a tiny fibrillation in the air between us, and I saw a tiny movement of his lips as I watched him make his sums inside his head. And he shook his head, and said, If you ever come near me again I'll call the Guards. And what will you tell them? I asked, and he had no answer, because there was none.

One evening of the Sabbath day I settled myself at the bar of a pub in West Limerick. The dry afternoon hour was still in force that time and the doors weren't long open. There was no casual customer there, only the hard core, the dependants, ranged along the counter grimly. I wasn't known from Adam in that place. I took my time about a pint of stout. Then I folded my newspaper onto the counter and wiped my lips with the back of my hand in a way I never would have done in company. I looked over at the pinched, sun-starved, late-middle-aged woman behind the bar and felt the intensity of her wondering about me wafting from her like a pungent breeze; it almost had a smell, a taste, that craving for knowledge about the intimate things in others' lives that consumes some people and radiates out from them.

Lord, it's a fright, I said. What does be going on? And I gestured to my closed paper. What's that now? the woman asked. A few faces turned towards me and away again; my gaze was fixed on the landlady, she was my quarry and my prize. Arra you know, I said, allowing an inflection into my speech that would be familiar to her, that would put her at ease, and in turn ease my story's passage to belief, its sublimation into cold fact. All that carry-on with children, all that, all that, *abuse*. It's all starting to come out now, isn't it? It's all coming home to roost now for the doers of evil. And she looked me now square into my eyes and I looked back and didn't blink. Doers of evil, I thought. Too much. But I had her all the same. Oh, there's a place they'll all be going to, she said, and you and I both know what it's called. We do, I said, we do. And I drank deeply from my stout as she poured a whiskey chaser for a crooked bristly man at the end of the bar whose eyes were darting and whose ears were cocked. The scary thing, I said to her as she floated back my way, is it's everywhere. Look at that man, you know him, he has a house built not a million miles from here, that's up for interfering with a girl no older than his own daughter, a girl from his daughter's class in school, I think, Lord Almighty, what would you do?

She stood in front of me and leaned close to me. There was a smell of Pond's cream and onions from her. Someone from around here? She was whispering. She was breathless with excitement. Her face reddened; it throbbed with colour, a scorching fever. She shrieked suddenly, FROM AROUND HERE? An old campaigner at the far end of the bar mishandled his glass in shock. Lord Jesus, who? Who? Who? And the hard core were suddenly breathless, deathly, not a drop passed a lip, not an eye blinked. And I pursed my lips and lowered my head and looked to my left and right as though checking for agents of the person about to be denounced, and a name slid softly from my mouth. I finished my stout in two or three slow tips of my glass and bade them all a good evening and, tapping the side of my nose, slipped from my high stool and left.

I had the world of research done before I drove out west that Sunday evening and drank that pint. Which public house was patronized by the least affiliated clientele, least bound by the strictures of association and its attendant senses of loyalty and circumspection, with the least to lose and the most to gain in pleasure by the having and spreading of a story. What was the best time to go there. Where was the best place to sit. Who best to address. And all this discovered fragmentarily, without anyone recognizing my motive. My story, my something out of nothing, replicated itself like a monster virus, mutating to strengthen itself, rearranging its component parts and properties to better survive each retelling and gain in size and virulence: it leaped the border into Kerry; it travelled back the road into Limerick City; it forded the estuary to Clare.

You can make something out of nothing, Father. I always knew this, even when the Christian Brothers were wearing out leathers hammering the first and second laws of nature into us. Energy can't be created or destroyed. Matter can't be created or destroyed. Only changed from one form to another. Bullshit. You can make a thing out of nothing, as true as God. I'm vindicated now by science too, you know, too late. They can create vacuums now that they examine with microscopes where the world we can't see is magnified a trillion times and they've found particles that appear all of a shot out of nowhere and disappear again. Out of nothing, into nothing. I used to read about all that stuff, until recently. The workings of nature, the makings of the world. They brought me some kind of a stand to prop my books up but it doesn't work great and so all I can do now is think. And sure, what harm? What harm is right.

People remember their lessons, though. That something can't come of nothing. Especially the very minute they hear a bad thing said about their neighbour. Yerra no, I don't know, they'll invariably say first, to make a show of loyalty. Sure, that couldn't be true. But then later they'll think about that thing they heard about the person and think, But why is it being said at all? Where has it come from? There has to be something at the bottom of it. Without even knowing it they'll think of what they were taught in school and what nature itself has bred into all men's minds: all things must come of other things; nothing can come from nothing. And once a thing enters a person's mind, it's always there, like woodworm in the leg of a chair, like cells of cancer, like rats in the cavities of the earth; it can't ever be fully eradicated. Even things long forgotten remain in the dark infinity of the mind; there's no unlearning. What's said can't be unsaid. And no law in this universe is immutable.

I bore false witness against that man, that neighbour of mine, and he came to me in my office in Augustine Stritch's converted townhouse and he told me he'd take the money after all: he wanted just to up his sticks and leave, to educate his children overseas; that way they'd speak another language, or know something of the wider world. That's a pity now, I said, you're just a week or so too late, the offer's off the table, the project plans have all been dropped. But maybe they'll be resurrected now, he said, now that I'm willing to help? And I told him I would see, and to go on about his work as normal, to hold off on any decisions relating to that certain project, that the terms would be different now, and I saw his eyes were threatened by tears as he nodded, his hands were shaking and he seemed to have shrunk; his face was drawn and his shirt and jacket billowed out around him as he walked. Come back to me a week from tomorrow, I said, and when he did I told him an account had been set up, and here were the keys and the codes, and as soon as he signed off on his decision and my clients were furnished with evidence of this, one hundred thousand pounds would be credited to that account. And he didn't even argue: he hadn't the heart.

Still I can't say it. I can't say what I was. I'll say what I looked to be to other people. An accountant. Then a lobbyist. I was given that title only years later, though. There was no official word for what I did until recently enough, though it's an ancient art. I arranged things for people. I read people well, and always knew the right words. I calculated people well and always knew the right amounts. Augustine Stritch gave me my start, and I took to numbers, their definiteness, their unyielding natures: even when you chop a number down to a half or a tenth or a millionth or a billionth part of its former self it still exists, it's still whole and pristine and incorruptible. When everything else is gone, when the universe has collapsed back in on itself and time itself has stopped, there'll still be numbers, frozen in the singularity, waiting for existence to push itself into being again, so they can put order on the great expansion, and tell it when it's reached its terminal mass, its ineluctable point of return to its beginning.

I was asked to present ideas, to persuade people to make certain decisions. That became the thing I was. Lobby is a strange verb. It keeps its shape and strangeness in conjugation, but it almost stops being a word. It becomes a soft sound with no meaning, no plosive part to give it an edge on utterance that it can tie itself to and make itself understood. I lobby, you lobby, he lobbies, I lobbied. I looked it up in a dictionary one time, to know its official meaning. To petition. I often had to repeat it in conversation. You what? A lobbyist. Oh, right, ya. The hiss in its tail as it became a noun would harden it and the syllables would meld sufficiently that the interlocutor would recognize the word and, after a few seconds of panicked thought of halls and porches and vestibules, they'd nearly always blush a little or cough nervously and excuse themselves with polite mumbles. I didn't even know it was what I was until a journalist called me it one time. The word often puts me in mind of a hand or a fist being drawn back and flung forward repeatedly to lend physical force to a position, to better deliver an argument, to ask for something with a hint of a threat. It puts others automatically in mind of lies.

Anyway, there was nothing, it seemed, that I couldn't get done. No plans I couldn't have brought to fruition, no White Papers I couldn't have transformed to law, no land I couldn't see bought or sold or parcelled or changed from green to red on council maps: whole towns rose up from the soil with the energy of my whispered words, my unbreakable promises, the grip of my enveloping hand. This was a new kind of a thing in people's minds, but discredited nearly before its birth, like the child of a prostitute. I was among the first, anyway, if not the first, to be given the title. I wasn't the first one, though. Wasn't Jesus Christ Himself petitioned as He starved and thirsted in the desert? The envelope He was offered contained the world.

O Father, bless me, I have sinned. O Father, hear me just. Hear me. I can't say it. I'll tell you instead about a man I once knew. A man, a kind of a tramp, I suppose, who stayed in a garret at the top of the building I lived in when I was first indentured to the Brothers Stritch. I don't know if he even paid rent. All I knew then was that at some point he'd lost something or someone and the loss had shattered him. Where, where, where? he'd say. Just that one word, over and over, a question to himself, to the world, to nobody. I'd meet him in the morning on the stairs or down in the damp hallway and he'd greet me with a whispered where or two, just as another person would say hello or good morning. Sometimes in the evenings he'd have drink taken or whatever calming drugs he was on would have worn off and he might pause as he passed to grip my forearm gently and his febrile eyes would meet mine; his wheres then would be louder, more urgent and imploring. I don't know, I'd reply, and shrug him off, hardly slowing. I often saw him at the end of town where I worked, standing with his back against the wall beside the Augustinians' vaulted doorway, an empty cardboard cup in one hand. He'd have his arms out slightly from his sides, one barely shod foot hiked up, his head resting against the concrete, his Adam's apple bobbing rhythmically as his breath was fashioned into a stream of low wheres by a soft ululation of his tongue and the barest rise

FROM A LOW AND QUIET SEA

and fall of his chin. Where, where, where flowing relentlessly through gapped and gritted teeth, like a never-ending, whispered prayer. As I passed him he'd show no sign of recognizing or even seeing me. His racked face would invariably be cast skyward, his pose fixed in a parody of the Passion, a casual crucifixion. I learned later from the landlord, who I think was related to him in some way but didn't care to admit it, that he'd lived years before in some roiling place in the centre of London and that he'd been married there. His infant son had toddled through an unlocked door and into the street. He was never found. He had searched and searched for a year and had lost his mind. He picked up a child once on a London street that looked like his son. It took seven or eight policemen to extricate the boy from his arms. The parents pushed for prosecution. He was sectioned, locked away for years, and repatriated on release. Hollowed, emptied, sent sailing home, at Her Majesty's pleasure and expense. I never put money in his cup. He never met my eye on the street. I thought nothing of him then, but I think of him often now.

I was married in 1970 at the age of twenty-five in the same church at Ardnamoher where I failed to make my first confession. I never failed again, though I never made an honest confession until today. I reeled the Act of Contrition off my tongue the second time of asking and each time after and most times he'd say, Good lad, go on, good lad, and he'd leave me away with two Hail Marys and a Glory Be. He'd sussed that I was who I was, from important people, from land. If he'd known that the first day he'd never have refused my absolution. I made up sins to tell that priest and all who came after him, and never mentioned the actual articles, the blasphemy or avarice, the vainglory or the lust. The terrible hubris. The other things. He was old, though, he couldn't keep us all straight in his head, us progeny of labourers and landed men and layabouts: the outward signs of a child's provenance were less distinct by then; everyone had shoes for one thing. I was married on a Friday morning and we had our wedding breakfast in O'Meara's Hotel in Nenagh and my father made no speech and her father stood to thank the reverend father and to acknowledge the efforts of my parents and to express his satisfaction at the mettle and manners of his new son-in-law. He was practised and perfunctory and he neglected to mention his daughter or his wife. They sat straight and silent, side by side, smiling coldly. I thought to stand and toast her beauty and her gentle nature but I couldn't. She was no beauty and anyway I hardly knew her. She was from unassailable, unimpeachable stock. She was from land that bordered ours. She was thick-hipped and thin-lipped and healthy. She gave me no trouble. She gave me three daughters and no son. And at the age of forty-five I fell in love.

I stayed sometimes in Limerick in a flat above a shop. I owned the building and the shop was leased to a cobbler and I liked to wake to his tapping hammer and the squeaking ratchet of his vice, to listen to the accents of his customers, the easy lilt of them. There was an open fire in the flat and I was careful to have the flue cleaned regularly so I could make use of it. I liked to write out plans and calculations on sheets of unlined paper, to plot courses and link people and places and events and contingencies together and then to convert my maps to lists of actions, and I'd commit the list of actions to memory and burn the sheet of paper in the fire. And this ritual became a sacred thing. I'd watch the paper blacken and light, and I'd watch the flames consume my plans, baptize them to smoke, and the smoke would be drawn upwards and out into the damp air. I dined some evenings in the restaurant of a hotel on the city's north side, a good walk along the river and across the bridge from my flat, and one Monday evening in the spring of 1990 I was served by a girl with blonde hair and light blue eyes and her hair was drawn back tightly from her face and tied in a braid, and her nose and lips and cheeks and chin were formed so perfectly they seemed impossible, like she was only a likeness of herself, a false image of perfection rendered by a flattering master. She asked me could she take my order in a soft accent that had the lilt but not the harshness of the city and I couldn't answer her for a long moment because I'd forgotten what I'd decided to have, I'd forgotten even what the choices were, or what I'd had the last time I'd been there, and I think if I'd had to give her my own name at that moment that I'd have failed. She smiled and asked if I needed a few more minutes and I recovered myself sufficiently to order a sirloin steak, medium rare, and I wondered at myself, at my foolishness, at this imposturous, impossible feeling, this sudden weakness that was after overtaking me. She came back my way to clear a table just vacated and I looked at the back of her neck and the backs of her arms and I thought I would pay any amount of money to be allowed to stand behind her and to touch my lips to the back of her neck, to put my hands on her arms and grip her gently, to press myself against her. She turned and saw me staring and she fumbled and dropped a plate and it smashed across the polished hardwood floor and she said, Fuck, fuck, and I laughed and she looked up at me from her pretty haunch and said, Sorry, I didn't mean to say fuck in front of a customer, and I told her she could say fuck in front of me any time, and that was the first time I'd ever used that kind of language in the presence of a member of the opposite sex and the sound of it from her and the sound of it from my own mouth thrilled me into the very centre of myself, into my tattered filthy soul.

I went there every evening that week. Earlier, so the dining room was quieter, and she was always there. I became very aware of myself: I'd always dressed smartly and subtly in dark, well-cut suits and Italian leather shoes but I started to worry at my hair in the bathroom mirror before leaving my flat, combing it and coiffing it and teasing out the grey, and I ran my razor round the inside of my nose, and I flossed my teeth and dabbed myself behind the ears with aftershave, like a woman, like a fool. And every evening she served me and she always seemed happy to see me, and she laughed at my jokes, and the sound of her laugh was soft, gorgeous. And my wife rang me on the Thursday at Stritch's and asked when I'd be home, and there was a querulous but not a quarrelsome tone to her voice, and she reminded me that Vigil Mass on Saturday was her mother's cousin's month's mind and that we'd be expected to go, and she had a parish committee meeting that night and I shouted suddenly, so loudly I could hear the outer office fall silent, THAT'S YOUR OWN BUSINESS, NOT MINE, and she took it well, God bless her, and she kept her voice even and she said, You don't normally give the whole week in the city, I just wondered was everything okay, were you under terrible pressure, and I can see now that you are, and I don't especially need to go to the meeting, and if I do decide to go I'm sure I can trust Olivia to mind the other two, she is fourteen now for pity's sake, she's big and bould enough to do it. And I felt a tenderness towards her then I'd never felt before, a gentle wave of something approximating love, and I thanked God for her, for her docile, passive nature, and I heard the waitress from the hotel in my head saying, Fuck, fuck, and I saw her on her haunches with her hand full of shards, and in my mind a shard had pierced her skin and a thin line of blood rivered along her palm and I took her hand in mine and examined her wound and I put her wound to my lips and her blood was warm and sweet and my wife was saying, John, John, are you there or are you gone? and I mumbled an apology, a story about a deal, a client, dinners, early starts, and I hung up on her and listened to the whispers from the juniors and the secretary, and I waited for Augustine to march through the door of my office demanding to know what the blazes I meant by that shouting, but he a hotel in Spanish Arch and we stayed there for a night and a day and another night and half a day, and I rang my wife and told her I'd been called to Dublin, to help a client through a crisis with his bank, and it was one of our biggest clients and so I couldn't really refuse, and she sounded weary on the phone and I could see her, lipless and harried, clutching the receiver white-knuckled, standing her ground against panic, against suspicion, against acceptance of the obvious conclusion, against the temptation to cause a scene, to profane, to step outside our hollow temple. And we drove back to Limerick and I dropped her at her shared house and I told her I loved her, and I meant it, and she said she loved me, and I think she meant that too, just as she said it.

I was good for a while, a good person, kind. For months and months I did my work and served my clients well, and any representations I made were heartfelt, and I swerved around the tricky cases, the problems insoluble except by dint of lucre. A man who'd been audited and found to be in breach of his fiscal duties and landed with a ruinous liability and fine came to me hat in hand, head hanging, and I told him not unkindly that if he'd come to me in the first place he'd never have been audited, let alone held liable for such a sum. He wished to have his case reviewed, he said, he had a small bit set aside, in case, in case. I explained to him the procedure to apply for lodging an appeal, but he already knew that. I thought you could, you know . . . lobby on my behalf, he said. And I said, Lobby? As though I'd never heard the word before. I held my office door open for him and I wished him all the best. I went home to my wife and daughters one week night and every weekend. I brought them little gifts. My wife had taken up charismatic prayer, whatever in the hell that is, I still don't know, and my

I wasn't practised at being in love. I tried to make her leave her job; I hated thinking of her serving anyone but me, of other men giving her glad eyes, pressing their sweaty gratuities into her hand, groping her, inhaling her, pitching their low-voiced proposals, of the chefs or the waiters or the greasy manager ogling her, of people looking at her on the street. I wanted her on my couch in my flat, in front of the fire, dressed only in the glow of it, waiting for me. I tried to tell her how it was for me, how I was under tremendous pressure, to be successful, to make money, to be certain things; I told her I could keep her for as long as she wanted me to. Keep me? she said. What does that mean? Own me? And I said, No, no, just do things for you to make your life easier, arrange a flat for you in a nice part of town, I could give you money for yourself, a regular amount, for spending, you'd have no rent to pay, buy you nice things. You could live here with me in this flat. I could be here most nights. Jesus, she said, I didn't really believe men like you existed. I thought men like you were made up. And I wasn't sure if she meant this in a good or a bad way.

I started to sit in my car down the quay from the house she lived in, a Georgian red-brick broken into bedsits, to see if she left for work alone and came home alone, to see if I could catch her in a lie. And after a week or so of this I saw her holding hands with a gangly tanned youth wearing skin-tight black

jeans and white trainers and a white T-shirt, and he was roped
with muscle and he was cocksure of himself, and I gripped the
steering wheel so tight my fingernails dug into the leather of
it and left little dents there, and I heard a sound escaping me,
a whiny breathless sound, and I felt the sting of tears in my
eyes for the first time since I could remember, since my dear
brother's funeral, I'd say, and I a middle-aged man with an
accountancy practice and a consultancy firm and a cash
fortune and a property portfolio and a new Jaguar and a solid
wife and solider daughters, and I found myself opening the
door of my Jaguar and stepping out onto the footpath and
standing with my hand on the top of the stone wall of the
quay, listening to the whispering river, and the sound it made
was you fool, you fool, you fool.

And I found myself at her door, and I found myself bang-
ing on it, and it was opened by the foreign-looking youth, and
he was scratching himself, staring at me. Who the fuck are
you? I said. Who the fuck am I? he said, in a Spanish accent,
or Portuguese. Is more like who the fuck are *you*? And she was
behind him suddenly, and she looked angry, and she was wearing a long T-shirt with *Bon Jovi* written on it and a picture
on it of a man with long hair and she was saying, It's okay,
Javier, it's my boyfriend, and she widened her eyes at him as
if to say, say nothing, and Javier turned his face to me and he
curled his lip into a sneer, and he looked me up and down
and said, *He* is a *boy*? And he was laughing as he rearranged
his private parts behind his blue Y-fronts, and suddenly I was
through the door and swinging and Javier was moving backwards and he was grinning still and he had a good reach and
a lightning swing and he caught me hard on the temple and
in the stomach, and I was winded and I was on the back foot

suddenly and I was falling and she was shouting, Jesus Christ, Javier, stop, just fucking stop, John, just leave me the fuck alone, and she pushed me out the door and slammed it in my face. And I stood there crying like a child awhile, and I drove home to my flat and my warm embers and I wondered at the things I hadn't known, the parts of myself I hadn't charted, my reckless, recondite nature. And that was all my dealings with adultery done.

Thou shalt not kill, it says in the Bible, the tendentious translation authorized by a man who let his own mother be killed so that he could be king. A man who thought himself divinely appointed. Kill is far too wide a word. *Lo tirzah*, God said at Sinai. Thou shalt not murder. I knew a man with LOVE on the knuckles of one hand and HATE on the knuckles of the other, and a series of dots along his wrists enumerating his convictions. I knew a man who knew this man, and I met the second man one evening on the street outside the cobbler's shop and the shop was locked and shuttered up and the narrow street door to my apartment was open and I had a stack of briquettes and a bag of coal and a bag or two of blocks arranged in the tiny foyer at the foot of the stairs because I was always cold that winter: I couldn't seem to warm myself or my empty flat, I couldn't seem to get back to myself at all. I gave the man who knew the man with the tattooed knuckles an envelope full of notes, a consideration for a favour I was asking of his friend, to pay a visit to a young Iberian and knock some small portion of the wind from his sails.

And I had a dream that night that I remember to this day, as though it were a thing that really happened, and happened only yesterday. In the dream I was walking past Youghalarra graveyard and down the hill towards the quay. In contrast with the glinting lake, there's a kind of darkness from the land down there, no matter how sunny the day. The sky may be clear and bright, yet a gloom will rise from the thick ditches and the dank brown reeds of the foreshore. Hulking evergreens line the road down to the quay and ring the sunless fields. It's as though the land absorbs and suffocates the light, while the water gives it life.

I stopped along the road at the gate of a house, a long bungalow, and there were people in the garden, drinking and eating; there was music being played but I couldn't see the musicians. A woman turned to me and she had sorrow in her eyes, and she said, A child is after going missing, a little boy, a child of this house. I looked away from her and saw that all of the guests from the party were darting about the roadway and the quay, shouting his name, peering into the water, searching the reeds and the undergrowth around the willows and the diving board, running over the rocks and along the sides of the crumbling boathouse. I walked up the lane that borders the foreshore, away from the road and the quay and the frantic crowd, along the forbidden route we always took as children. I came in sight of the little pebble beach known only to a daring few that lies at the end of a gently sloping bank, almost fully hidden from view by a copse of ash trees. A sand-bar forms a soft track, ankle-deep in the water of that bay within a bay, that's warm and pleasant on the soles and can lead the unwary outwards from the shallows towards open water. Only a short way from the shore the going becomes treacherous: the lakebed drops suddenly in places and the sands shift with sly currents and unseen eddies. Forests of reeds invite young explorers. Weeds like nests of vipers lie in wait in hidden hollows. And there I saw the child. He'd paddled out about twenty yards and must have slipped from the sandbar into deeper water and become tangled. His head was barely breaking the surface, bobbing desperately as he tried to free himself from the weeds' grip. I could just make out his eyes, wide with terror, as small waves lapped against his face. I could hear him splutter and choke; he was starting to inhale water. He hadn't breath enough to call out, though he must have heard his mother and father and all the others shouting his name just around the bend of the lakeshore. He was using one hand to keep himself up as best he could with a wild, flailing, outward stroke. He must have been reaching downwards with his other hand to the vicious tangle around his legs. I judged that he had a bare minute left of life, if even that. His arm would soon cede to exhaustion; those deadly little waves, mostly of his own making, would soon find ingress and swamp his lungs.

I stood tight in my dream to the cool trunk of an ancient ash tree, unseen in the dappling shadows of the muddy bank. I watched a mayfly light on a leaf to rest for a few seconds of his one eternal day. I wondered at the mayfly's sudden stillness, while the sounds of sobs and splashes faded from my mind. When it flew away, back towards the canopy of the looming trees, I stood squinting from the shade against the dancing shards of light on the water's surface, and, seeing that I could no longer see any part of him, ran from my hiding place, splashing wildly through the shallows, falling, rising, roaring, and the voices still were shouting out his name, and some of them were shouting Edward, and some of them were shouting Javier, and some of them were shouting John. I grabbed the glass-eyed boy, tearing the weeds from his legs as I lifted, and held him to my chest. His head flopped back, his limbs hung limp. His lips were blue, his face white; a thin river of lake water ran from the side of his open mouth. A bare crescent of pupil broke the whiteness of his eyes. I laid him on a soft bed of dead reeds on the foreshore and put my mouth over his; three breaths, thirty compressions of his chest, over and over, counting and crying, trying to force the foul water from him and make his heart beat again, to force the life back into him, to take back what I'd done. But time has only one direction, and I'd filled those blank moments after I first found him with nothing but the watching of the stillness of a mayfly. He wasn't moving, and would never move again, and whatever unsullied bit had been left on my soul was gone to black and the gates of Hell were flung open to me now in welcome. And I woke drenched and gasping, face-down on my double bed, and I knew before I heard the news the terrible thing that I had done.

I had to go to Brussels a few weeks later. We flew into violent air. Something in the plane's mechanical or electrical parts stopped working. The cabin lost pressure; oxygen masks popped out and hung in front of people's faces like yellow gibbets. The plane lurched up and down, and then started to descend at a lunatic angle. People were clutching each other and crying. Some were praying out loud. A baby screamed, squeezed too tightly by its white-faced mother. The pilot's crackling instructions were ignored, drowned by panic and a rising whine from the stressed turboprops. I sat still, watching the mask dancing before my eyes. I think I was smiling. There was a man across the aisle, the one age with me, the same kind of a go as me, you might say. We'd nodded at one another on boarding. I looked across at him as the rushing air outside shrieked over the plane's canted wings and the overhead compartments gaped open in unison and vomited coats, bags, bottles and boxes of fags all over passengers and the empty aisle. He was smiling too. And he said, in a soft, clear voice that I could easily hear in spite of the hysteria all around us: There'll be no pain, you know. If we go down, we'll just evaporate. Evaporate. He looked away from me again and put his right arm out to soothe a person I couldn't see in the window seat beside him.

And I felt calm and looked forward to being atomized,

released into vapour. The pilot pulled the sick bird up and landed it for a finish, with a terrific whump into the tarmac. Whatever had been knocked off by the turbulence had restarted just in time. There were some eardrums burst from the sudden drop, ribs broken from the hard landing, a few lacerations from flying duty-free, and a scattering of meely-mawlies in need of handholding and bottled oxygen from the shock of it all. Paramedics picked their way along the strewn aisle, checking and tending, before anyone was allowed to stir from their sodden seats. Fire trucks and ambulances were massed, circling slowly below us in frustrated redundancy, each like a pugilist at a cancelled bout, shadow-boxing in an empty ring. That man didn't speak to me again, but he looked at me with an expression I couldn't read just before we were evacuated. He had the bluest eyes I've ever seen.

The captain stood by the bulkhead near the top of the exit steps, dutiful and awkward. He looked too young to be in command of anything, let alone a planeload of lives. Women were hugging him before they disembarked, crying with joy, high and sick with relief. Pale men took his hand in both of theirs while he stood straight, flanked by two tousled beauties, smiling, apologetic, embarrassed. I looked back but I couldn't see the man who'd spoken to me. I wondered had I imagined him. I wonder that still. I walked out past the pilot without acknowledging him. People felt they'd cheated death that day. It was the other way round for me.

O my God, I am heartily sorry for having offended Thee, and I detest all my sins, because I dread the loss of Heaven, and the pains of Hell, but most of all because they offend Thee, my God, Who are all good and deserving of all my love.

Lake Islands

his eyes were bulging and it was one of those nights when the place was full but it was quiet, there was no match on or anything being argued about, and every fucker was only waiting for him to say something, as usual, or dredge up a yarn from somewhere, and poor Ad had stepped right into the spotlight and the whole place was skitting behind their hands and letting on to be not laughing at all and Mickey Briars didn't give a fuck, he was roaring laughing, knowing there was a flame after being lit that he could stoke and stoke, and Ad was taking it badly. There was shapes thrown. Dixie had had to hold his hands up and then hold his hand out, and explain how it was only something that had occurred to him there on the spur of the moment, and Ad had given the night sulking and telling Dixie and everyone else that that was how stories got out, that was how names got blackened, fuckers saying things like that, on the spur of the moment, and he was saying *on the spur of the moment* in a by-the-way imitation of Dixie's voice, like a right funny man, and for a finish Dixie had said, Ad, you're either letting it go or you're not, and he'd set his voice at just the right pitch, low and even, to let Ad know to drop it there. Or he could get a fucking smack. He'd left four bags of blocks at Ad's door the next day, just by way of pacifying him. Ad had thanked him graciously enough in Ciss's that night. They'd drunk a small one together. A bit of something had lingered, though, for all the making-up they'd done. A certain coldness, a quickness to argue, a slowness to laugh. It was the fucker's own fault anyway for never having married, nor even done a line for all anyone knew, and for living on his own and giving his days to looking out his window at children kicking football on the green. He wasn't there, anyway, and so Dixie hurried on. You'd never know when he'd pop out, like a long grisly Jack-in-the-box.

The council promise perennially to widen the gap and pave the foot-worn walkway through the field of scrub and briars to the commonage of the hill where every man is free to roam. Free. He spits each time he breaches the gap. They're all in league: the bigshots in the offices in town; the remnants of the Proddie crowd that used own half the land and the mountain with it; the posh knobs on the far side of the hill that wanted no riff-raff traipsing over hills and down valleys and through their delicate country. Like children dragging muck in along a carpet. Herbie Grogan took a look one time when there was an election on. Oh, yes, he said, oh, yes, I can see what you're saying. What a lovely amenity. A footpath would certainly add to it, allow it to be fully utilized. Isn't it well to have it, though, so close to your houses and everything? Wasn't it great planning all the same? The prick was nearly making out the hill was put there by the likes of him, dreamed up and proposed and voted on and dragged stone by stone from the earth and set pretty as a view for wasters, something for them to admire out the windows of their little houses. We gave you a house and we gave you a mountain, he was saying. Now is there any fear you'd shut your fucking mouth and put your mark beside my name on Friday week? You've a grand face for fancy paths.

The puffy clouds had given way to blue and the bit of snow that fell was hardening to a thin crust and there was a good couple of hours or so of daylight left. More on the far side of the hill, of course, where the big houses were, where the western horizon was lower and farther away. The quality, of course, as usual, allowing themselves every ease and privilege. The path that zigzagged up the hill was dry; what water fell there was soaked into the peaty ground or ran in culverts to a night were still untold, except to his daughter, but she didn't appreciate them, only lit always on the funniest bits and gave out about them, and damped the punchline always down to nothing, and ruined the stories, and he only told her them to practise the telling of them, because in fairness to the boy he appreciated a good story, he got a great kick out of some of the yarns he brought home from Ciss Brien's or the Half Barrel inside in town or the Frolics below in Carney. And he felt foolish now at his own excitement, his childish joy since the minute he woke this morning at his triumph over Hughie Fitz last night in Ciss Brien's, and everyone telling Hughie he was gorgeous in the new coat Bridget bought him for his birthday, and every cunt telling him how they couldn't believe he was sixty, and making out they wouldn't have given him a day over fifty, and the pure delight on Hughie's face when Dixie'd seemingly joined in and compared him to your man George Clooney, and the tide of purple that had risen up along Hughie's neck when he'd taken it back and said he meant Mickey Rooney, and the way Podge had laughed so much behind the bar he'd had to stop what he was doing to draw his breath back and collect himself for a full minute at least, and the hard chaws from the Island Field that were out doing the steel fixing for the new railway bridge over in Lackanavea had bursted their arses laughing, and he'd timed it perfect, so he had, spot on to the millisecond, and it wasn't every man could time a slag so well. He'd try the boy again when he was in better humour.

Some stories a man could glory in. Some stories were told for kudos more than laughs. Like the one his mother used to tell him about the time she was fired from the kitchen of the house of the people who'd owned the land below him, spread along the gentle slope down to the lake, the guts of a thousand acres all in all, and even a mile of foreshore annexed, though such land by right was commonage, and never could be owned by just one man. She hadn't addressed him by his proper title, which was Lord, a title given him by succession on the death of some childless uncle in England, in Sussex or Essex or Wessex or some place like that. Call me Lord, he said, or so the story went, one day when she was bringing him his tea. I won't, sir, she replied. I have only one Lord, and He's watching from Heaven, and I'll never use His name in vain, nor ever will I give it to another. Get out then, old Manford said, get out of here and don't come back. And that was the forties. People still were expected to bow and scrape even then, and the country supposedly free. That man of the Manfords employed dozens of men, and paid each one of them late on a Saturday, the way no man would be tempted to slacken off before his full week's labour was given, and even when there was nothing to be done on the land or in the house they were made wait, and women who wanted to go to the shop to buy for the dinner next day were made wait, and the whole parish stood still and waited for the pleasure of his lordship, for the opening of his lordship's purse. His mother had left her job that day and walked the steep road home, back to her people in Glencrue. And the Manfords' house was now a shell, four storeys still but without roof or floor, and the steeple of their private church was lying where it fell, graved in moss and the shit of birds.

There were nights the boy stayed out. Dixie couldn't sleep those nights. He'd sit up in bed and turn the radio on low, or sometimes he'd read his books, and sometimes the words would swim on the page, and he'd steady himself and he'd slow his breathing down and he'd imagine the panic that rose inside him to be rising water against a lock gate, and he'd picture the wheel of the lock gate being turned, and he'd imagine the flow through the lock, the downward easing, the levelling. That was a trick he'd taught himself. Smart cunts charged fortunes for that kind of shite. Some nights the boy would arrive in ragged and cut from drink in the small hours, and he'd stomp around the kitchen making toast or what-have-you, and the sound of him home was a blessed sound, and he'd say, Well, Pop, if he chanced going down for a look at him, and once or twice he'd caught himself standing at the foot of the stairs in his pyjamas and slippers and dressing-gown, just standing there, looking in through the half-open door to the kitchen, looking at his grandson sitting at the table eating toast, the way a man might look at a child in a cradle, a soft man given to womanly emotions, and he'd catch himself admiring him, the strong jaw of him, the fine thick head of hair, the good-sized hands, and he'd catch himself thanking God for him, for delivering him home from the cold night.

He never could convert his love to words. He longed to hold the boy the way he used to, to fold him into himself, to hold him hard against him, saying, My boy, my boy. The foolishness that swept through him, more every day; it was like a rogue current below a flat, still surface, a deadly undertow that could drag you down to perdition. The day his daughter landed in with her news he'd surprised himself. Thank God your mother isn't here to see this day, he'd said, and watched his daughter's blue eyes fill with tears, and straight across the room he went to her, and he hadn't known until he was nearly across to where she was standing in the bay of the window would he hit her or hold her, or stand with his hands hanging made for him by his mother; he'd be in better form and a bit sheepish over earlier; he'd be willing to hear about the crack in the pub and the story of the cutting-down-to-size of Hughie Fitz. And his heart sank back at the realization that it wasn't Lampy at the table, it was his daughter's friend from the hospital, the brown-skinned, dark-haired lad, who called once in a wonder, and sat in near silence looking at his daughter, and she sat looking back at him, and he couldn't watch them at it, it was unbearable, and so he went out to his shed or up the hill or down the road to Ciss's whenever he came. He'd suffered terrible, Florence said, and he was here on licence, and he was a locum, and Pop didn't know what that was and nor did he ask. Every foreigner had a story, a lament, and they had all to be taken with a pinch of salt or, even better, not at all. He wondered how it would go at Ciss's if Florence married a foreign Johnny, after all the jokes he'd heard cracked there and all the jokes he'd cracked himself and all the talk along the years about keeping them out, about there not being jobs enough for the Irish, about there not being space enough for all the madding hordes. Fuck them, he thought. It'd nearly be a pleasure telling them. The loudest mouths of all were the ones who'd never done a hand's turn their whole lives. He slowed himself to ease the creaking of the gate, and he kept to the grass to the right of the garden path the way he wouldn't be spotted passing back to his shed. He'd plug the Dimplex in and settle himself in the old armchair and he'd smoke a fag or two and read the pile of papers from the week. Leave them at it, looking into one another's eyes.

From her seat at the kitchen table Florence saw her father at the gate. She hoped he'd go straight to his shed. Farouk was talking today, more than he had ever done, and she felt he was about to say something, about his wife or his daughter or his faraway home, about what had happened to him, about his heart, his poor heart. She knew his story, as everyone at the hospital did, from the first day he worked there as a locum: Freda Wiley from HR had spread the contents of his file and his life around the wards and the corridors before she went on her break that morning. Florence had only to allocate his parking space and print his permit and his identification badge, and he'd sat across from her in her tiny office as she'd threaded a lanyard through the badge, and she'd looked at him and seen that he was smiling at her and so she smiled back, and she'd told him to call in to her any time at all if he needed anything, or had any problems with his parking or his email or his post or anything else, and she knew from his file that he was forty-four, but he looked younger; he had a boyish gait, a kind of a loose-limbed way of moving, though his hair at the sides was shot with streaks of grey, and his eyes were dark and shrouded.

She wonders at herself sometimes. Why she wants so badly for this man to speak to her. Why it matters that he tells her all his truths, when she holds her own so tightly to herself. He talks and she listens and she studies his eyes. She understands only a little of what he says sometimes. He tamps reality down, he says. The universe could be contained on a pinhead. Elementary particles have no interior structure, did you know that? And she shakes her head, no, she didn't know that. And he laughs, a low, gentle laugh that could break easily to a sob but never does. She gets the feeling he hasn't cried for a long while, years maybe, that he's armoured himself against the truth of things with theories and explanations and ways of persuading himself that nothing ever happened. He's allowed himself to lose his mind. It's easy then to tamp reality down and down to nothing, he says. If an elementary particle has no interior structure or any outer shell, then what is it but nothing-ness, and so we are made from nothing, and so is the universe, and all of this – he casts his hand at the ceiling, at her, back at himself – is nothing. A dream, maybe. But we are not the dreaming, we're the dreamed. And he laughs again and she doesn't know what to say. Do you know what some boys called me on the street yesterday? Shit-face. Go home, shit-face, they said. Go home to fuck. Go home to fuck, they said. Can you imagine saying that? Can you imagine what happens in their minds? And all I could think to do was laugh. What else is there to do? And she feels then she should be soothing him, somehow, shushing him, stroking his face and hair and urging him in a low whisper to sleep; she imagines herself lying beside him, pressed against him, and she's surprised at herself, at the sudden stab she feels, of longing, of terrible want.

He'd come to her office one day, a week into his second locum stint at the hospital, before he started his rounds in the wards, and he'd asked her in a faltering voice, in clipped un-even words, so low she could barely hear him, if she'd like to come with him for a drive that weekend, to the sea. And she'd been so shocked she'd paused too long before answering, and he was turning away towards the door before she said, Yes, yes, that'd be lovely, and he'd smiled at her and said, Good. I drive to the sea when I can, he said. And sometimes it feels so lonely there.

And he'd collected her in an old Mercedes, and the radio kept coming on of its own accord, at full volume, startling them, and they laughed each time it happened, and their laughter and the spasmodic radio filled the hour it took them to get to Lahinch, and it was twenty years since she'd walked that beach, and the last man she'd walked it with had been handsome too, and full of mystery, and he'd pulled her down onto the sand and kissed her hard. Farouk would never do that, she knew. But at the tideline they'd stood side by side looking out at the churning sea, and he'd reached for her hand and held it, and she'd felt through his palm the pulse of his pounding heart.

They drove together often after that. Even when he was assigned elsewhere, to Limerick or Ballinasloe or Ennis, he'd text her, short messages, unpunctuated, WILL U COME FOR DRIVE SUN 3PM, and she'd reply YES, and he'd always be a few minutes early and Pop would humph and grunt out through the blinds, and ask why he wasn't coming in, and she'd say, Maybe he doesn't feel very welcome, Dad, and he'd pretend offence and say, Lord Almighty, what has a man to do? Roll out a red fuckin carpet for every cunt? And she'd say Farouk was from a culture with a welcome imperative, where even your enemy was afforded your hospitality in your house, and he'd say, Welcome imperative my bollix, that's all very well until they're flying planes into skyscrapers and chopping every cunt's head off for saying the wrong prayers. And she'd say, DAD! and she'd shake her head, but she knew what he really meant, what his fear really was, because she knew the truth of her father well, the warm and wounded heart of him.

She went about each day the same way. Waking early and listening to the singing birds. Listing in her head the things to be done. Deciding on her outfit and her shoes, her bracelet and earrings. Whether she needed to stop on the way to the hospital for petrol or on the way home for messages. What she'd cook for Dad and Laurence for their tea. What she'd have for her lunch; whether the rain would hold off so she could go for her walk at lunchtime, across Sarsfield Bridge and down along the quays and past the courthouse and back around to Thomond Bridge and up again full circle to the hospital's back gate; whether Freda Wiley would go walking with her, chattering non-stop about this one or that, what was said and what was said back, and who had turned around and done or said what to whom and she would hmm and nod and laugh and pretend disgust at the appropriate times and Freda loved to talk, she hardly drew breath in the effort to fit in as much as she could to the time of their walk, and so no gap would be allowed, no lull, no silent space that might allow into Florence's mind a trickle of blood from Javier's nose, and from the side of his mouth, and from the cut above his eyebrow, and his bulbous blackened eyes, and his slack buckled body heaped in the corner and the men standing over him looking, one of them saying, Fuck, fuck anyway, is he dead? and the man with his arm around her throat whispering into her ear all the things he was going to do to her, and the hardness of him sticking in her back, and his laughing as she struggled to be free, and the paramedics kneeling, glancing,

Mrs Coyne is happy. The handsome young therapist is telling her again the same thing he told her on her last visit. To sit up in bed first, and then to swing her legs out, and to sit on the edge of the bed and to start with her toes. Wiggle them, wiggle them. Then to lift her heels and press the balls of her feet downwards. To count slowly to ten, or until she feels heat flowing into her calves. Then to dig her heels into the floor and exert pressure downwards to stretch the muscles in the fronts of her legs. Count slowly to ten again. And on you go with this, up along your body to your arms and neck until your blood is warmed and flowing and your muscles are all ready for the day. Don't stand up until you're sure you won't fall down. She wonders if he's forgotten or if he presumes she'll have forgotten. She doesn't care either way. There's a beautiful smell off of him. He's kneeling on the floor in front of her and she's on a hard chair with the foot he's working on raised and rested on a low padded stool and the consulting room is empty but for them and the door to the corridor is closed. She leans herself forward as far as she can, gripping the armrests tight to hold herself, to stop herself falling forward on top of him. Can you imagine? He'd get some hop. A woman sixty years his senior landing on top of him. She's nearly close enough to smell his hair. He has lovely hair, thick and fair, tousled a bit like he hadn't time to comb it. Probably he hadn't. They're very understaffed in all these places. You'd need to go private now for a therapist with nicely combed hair. She's just about to breathe in the scent of him when he looks up at her and smiles. He has blue eyes, shining with kindness, and a wide mouth full of straight white teeth. He has a funny kind of a foreign accent. Not Australian, quite. Nor not American at all. Definitely not English, though it is quite refined. He has a name you couldn't put with a country too easily. She closes her eyes and searches for it, and it's right there in the front of her mind, dancing away from her each time she gets close. David. David. That's his first name. A name she always liked. Dear one, it means. Vorster. That's the surname. Vorster. And he's from South Africa, she suddenly remembers. And the sound of that country always puts her in mind of supermarket checkouts, and fruit, and pickets, and she can't fully remember why that should be. Something years ago, something that was in the news.

She knows Australian accents well. That's how she was able easily to rule out the therapist being from there, even before she asked him. Several times she had visits from grand-children. Backpacking, they said they were. Around the world. She didn't know how it was done. One lad came a couple of years ago and he stayed a fortnight or so, a fine tall lad, and he went off down the town one night and didn't come home until the sun was up and when he did she was asleep in the kitchen chair waiting for him, because she'd been terrified something had happened to him, and she read him the Riot Act there in the kitchen and he'd said, Chill out, Gran, chill out, and still for all his smartness he'd looked sheepish and he'd told her he was sorry, he hadn't realized she'd be so worried, and he said he'd walked a sheila home who lived out in the boondocks; that was his way of saying out in the countryside and she'd had to stop herself laughing at the sound of it, the way he wouldn't know she wasn't really as cross as she made out, only so relieved to see him, and he'd gotten kind of lost on his way back, and she'd said, Lord bless us, Sheila who? And he'd laughed at her and she'd laughed at herself, and they were very pally after that once he'd explained himself a bit and promised not to be gallivanting down around the town until all hours. He'd shown her his computer thing, a tablet he called it, and a thing you could press on to go into pictures of people, and he showed her all sorts of people and children and babies and they were all relations of her but she couldn't hold them in a line in her head in a million years, and he came to a photograph of a big round man with a baldy head and bright-coloured shorts standing holding a fish out beside him that was nearly the length of himself, and he'd said Grandad caught that in the Worra Worra or somewhere with a funny name like that, a river she presumed, and she'd gotten a terrible shock at the realization that the old man in the picture was her son and that this tall boy who was a half a step or less from man-hood wasn't her grandchild at all but her great-grandchild.

The same lad sent her a package the next Christmas. There was a box in it with an apple on the front of it with a bite taken out of it. There was a machine in the box the very same as the one he'd shown her all the pictures on. There was a card with a kitten on the front of it in a Santy hat and inside was written, Stay in touch, G-Gran, love you, Mark. And she'd puzzled at the extra G for ages before she'd arrived at the answer: Great-Gran. And she'd laughed, and she remembered his voice well, deep but not long broken, and she could hear her saying it in her mind, and she'd held the card to her lips and to her and he seems to make no sharp sounds, to have no way about him that isn't gentle, and the bed is a narrow mattress with a gleaming white sheet tight across it and no yield in it, and she closes her eyes while he rubs and softly kneads at her muscles, and teases the stiffness out from her joints, and she imagines herself reaching up and closing her hand on the collar of his shirt and pulling him down onto her and the feeling of his lips on hers, of his body on top of hers, and she laughs suddenly at the thought of it, at what he'd think of her if he knew what was in her mind, and he says, Sorry, Mrs Coyne, am I tickling you? And the way he says *you* is so lovely, lilted and drawn out, and there's a funny slant to his smile and a gleam in his blue eyes and she's certain sure for a moment that he knows, he knows exactly what has been going on inside her old head.

She used to type things into Google now and then. One day she typed in HEAVEN. She saw pictures of angels and crosses and clouds and rays of light shining down from blue skies. It was there, so. The way she'd imagined it. Another day she typed in WHAT HAPPENS WHEN YOU DIE. You will return to dust, the internet said. And it said, As soon as you die, every muscle in your body relaxes. And it said plenty of other things too but she hadn't the heart for them, all the voices, and she'd noticed people cursed at one another a lot on the internet, if you looked down into the discussions people had that were below nearly every story you read. You can send them a friend request, you know, her neighbour said. So they'll know you're there, your grandchildren and everyone. And you'll be able to have conversations with them and all their pictures and stories will show up in a list automatically when you log in. Arra, that's the last thing they'd want, she said. To know there's an oul one watching them from half a world away. And spin back to the home and to put him back in his box a bit, though she wouldn't be too sour with him because you never know what sort of hardships people might have gone through in their lives, and the boy of the Shanleys is smiling at her as he reaches for her hand to help her onto the step at the side of the bus, and there was a ferocious sense of sadness off of that boy, always, and she dimly remembers something about his mother, about something terrible happening to her before he was born, but the story is jumbled into a thousand others, and she watches him sometimes while she knits in the day room, and she feels a warm and foolish thrill when his face creases to laughter at the things she says sometimes, the few swipes and cuts she takes at the ones deaf and doting around her, and she feels like saying to him, Don't worry, my dear, don't be wasting your time worrying, the day is only a dream away that you'll be sitting here where I am looking over at a boy like you and wondering how are you all of a sudden so old, where did all the years go, and he reminds her of her own son, how he was always worried about something, how he was never settled or easy in himself, how he and his father could never get on but were forever flinting and sparking off of each other and threatening to ignite and combust, and how Maurice had gone to Australia in a fit of crossness, and how his father had waited and waited for him to come back, and his heart solid broken, and he never had.

And she says to Lampy Shanley now, Have we to go to Milford or are we going straight home? And the boy of the Shanleys looks puzzled at her and says, Why would we go to Milford? And she says, Weren't you to drop the man in the wheelchair at Milford? The man that was in the very back of the other bus? You'll surely to God be collecting him? And

And Lampy Shanley's grandfather is sitting in his shed with his Dimplex going full wallop against the marching cold, sucking his fag to the burned lip, resting his eye on the curve of a page-three girl. And his mother is sitting at her kitchen table with her right hand resting gently on the top of the left hand of her friend Farouk, and Farouk's eyes are cast downwards as he speaks, and he's telling her a story of a girl, who was captured by a king, who locked her in a tower. And Lampy is holding the thin warm hand of Mrs Coyne and the freezing air is still and the steam of her words is wisping gently heavenward and she's standing on the hydraulic step now and she's stopped moving and she's looking at him, and a memory is forming itself clearly in Lampy's mind, a recent memory of words spoken, an echo forming itself back into its original shape and volume, words spoken by a squat and harried nurse, while he was dreaming about Chloe or Eleanor or whether he should have a wank before he goes out tonight, words of admonishment to James Grogan, about the risk he was taking with people's lives, with his reputation, with all their livelihoods, letting the young boy handle patients on his own, that the man in the wheelchair needed a nurse to accompany him, that the ramp itself was tricky to get right, that the view from the front of the bus was blocked by the bulkhead, that he could choke, or, or . . .

And there's a man kneeling on the floor beside the empty wheelchair, and he's pitched forward and his head is bowed, and he's resting his hands on the seat next to the wheelchair, the seat where a nurse or a care assistant should have been sitting when the bus had left the care home earlier that frosty day, and the fingers of his hands are clamped together, and his aspect is that of a man giving his confession, a penitent, a seeker of forgiveness, and Florence Shanley doesn't recognize this man, he's had two strokes and twenty years have passed since they lay together, and his eyes are closed and what can be seen of his face is white and his lips are blue and he's been dead at least an hour.

And Farouk Alahad pauses before the kneeling man before he puts his fingers to the spot above his clavicle where his pulse would be most easily detectable, so he can say for certain that he's dead, and he can give a time in his statement, and he can give true evidence that he checked the man's vital signs, though it was obvious that he was frozen and could not be alive. And for a moment he envies the dead man his easy end. Below a certain threshold of temperature the brain inverts the sensation of cold and a body feels warmth and a strange comfort as its energy dissipates. That's why men lie down in snow and die. And then he feels a hand in his, and the hand is warm, and he feels through her palm the pulse of her pounding heart.

And Lampy gets to where his grandfather is, and his mother, and her friend from work, whose name he can't remember, a foreign fella who drives an old shiteheap of a Merc, and he sees that his mother and the foreign fella are holding hands and he's happy for his mother, and he thinks of the slagging he's going to get at training; then he remembers he doesn't hurl any more, and the ambulance people are there already, and everyone now is still and they're all looking at him, and he knows then that the man is dead, and he sees that the body is shrouded, and the air is still but for the clouded breath of the people standing there, and Lampy feels the cold suddenly, down into the centre of himself, and a weakness in his legs so that he can hardly stand up, and just as he begins to fall his grandfather's arms are around him, and his arms are still strong, and he's holding his grandson tight, and he's saying, My boy, my boy, my boy.

Acknowledgements

Thanks:

To the people who read my books; to Brian Langan, Eoin McHugh, Fiona Murphy, Larry Finlay, Bill Scott-Kerr, Helen Edwards, Patsy Irwin, Sophie Christopher, Hazel Orme and everyone at Doubleday Ireland, Penguin Random House Ireland and Transworld UK; to Antony Farrell and everyone at The Lilliput Press; to Kathryn Court, Victoria Savanh, Christopher Smith and everyone at Penguin US; to Marianne Gunn O'Connor; to Joseph O'Connor, Tom Lodge, Claire Ryan, Sarah Moore Fitzgerald, Giles Foden, Julian Gough, Mary O'Malley and my colleagues, friends and students at the University of Limerick; to Billy Keane, Alan Hayes and all the offerers of kindness and support I've met along the way; to Garry Browne, Conor Cremin, Brian Treacy and all my neglected friends; to Ethel Hartnett, for the laughs; to Betty Sheehan and all the in-laws, out-laws, nearly-cousins, proper cousins and might-be cousins who help to make this life so rich; to my wonderful parents, Anne and Donie Ryan; to Mary, Christopher, Daniel, John, Lindsey, Aoibhinn and all my family near and far; to Thomas and Lucy, the brilliant lights of my life; and to Anne Marie, my true love, who made this book and all my books.

Donal Ryan is from Nenagh in County Tipperary. His first three novels, *The Spinning Heart, The Thing About December* and *All We Shall Know,* and his short-story collection *A Slanting of the Sun,* have all been published to major acclaim. *The Spinning Heart* won the Guardian First Book Award, the EU Prize for Literature (Ireland), and Book of the Year at the Irish Book Awards; it was shortlisted for the International IMPAC Dublin Literary Award; and longlisted for the Man Booker Prize and the Desmond Elliott Prize, and was recently voted 'Irish Book of the Decade'. A former civil servant, Donal lectures in Creative Writing at the University of Limerick. He lives with his wife Anne Marie and their two children just outside Limerick City.